HOLLOWHEART

BEN EADS

**Let the world know:
#IGotMyCLPBook!**

**Crystal Lake Publishing
www.CrystalLakePub.com**

WELCOME TO
CRYSTAL LAKE
PUBLISHING

TALES FROM THE
DARKEST DEPTHS

OTHER TITLES BY BEN EADS:

Cracked Sky

OTHER NOVELLAS BY CRYSTAL LAKE PUBLISHING

Every Foul Spirit by William Gorman
The Pale White by Chad Lutzke
A Season in Hell by Kenneth W. Cain
Quiet Places: A Novella of Cosmic Folk Horror by Jasper Bark
The Final Reconciliation by Todd Keisling
Wind Chill by Patrick Rutigliano
Little Dead Red by Mercedes M. Yardley
Sleeper(s) by Paul Kane

Or check out other Crystal Lake Publishing books for more Tales from the Darkest Depths.

Welcome to another Crystal Lake Publishing creation.

Thank you for supporting independent publishing and small presses. You rock, and hopefully you'll quickly realize why we've become one of the world's leading publishers of Dark and Speculative Fiction. We have some of the world's best fans for a reason, and hopefully we'll be able to add you to that list really soon. Be sure to sign up for our newsletter to receive some free eBooks, as well as info on new releases, special offers, and so much more.

**Welcome to Crystal Lake Publishing—
Tales from the Darkest Depths.**

PROLOGUE

MAKING DEALS WITH the dead had to stop.

Ever since Dalton had first met The Architect, his life moved like a cog in a rusted clock, ticking down the minutes to find the one who escaped what lived in the hollow. Dalton hoped this would be the last time he would meet with The Architect. The problem with peeking behind the curtain was the same as always—once seen, it could not be unseen. Curiosity becomes weaponized. From that moment on, you become a mechanism.

As Dalton drove to the hollow, for what felt like the millionth time, he hoped The Architect would accept his best friend, Terrell, instead.

Knowing the perverted shit you've been up to, I wouldn't even flinch.

It would be too easy to reach over his BMW's center console and strangle the fat fuck. Despite the BMW's large interior, Terrell's body touched Dalton's right arm, no matter how far he recoiled. His body odor stank of rotten fruit.

Every meeting, Dalton gave himself a good ninety-five percent chance of survival. Tonight? More like fifty-fifty. Even the Xanax that usually turned his head into a balloon did little to calm his nerves.

Focus. Focus. Stick to the plan.

Once the sun set, lights of homes and trailers blinked out in the rearview, as if winking at him, saying, "Good luck, buddy." Dalton's headlamps hit the weathered sign welcoming him and Terrell to Shady Hills, in the heart of Florida. He let off the gas, creeping toward the hollow. Gravel crunched under the tires, striking the sides of his once pristine car. Red and orange leaves slapped the windshield, whipped around by an early winter breeze.

Old, massive oaks and birches flanked the dirt road they turned on. Remembering the lavender smell of his daughter's hair, her infectious giggles, helped him focus.

Despite the car's heating system, the cold crept in between his ribs, caressing his lungs, his heart. He caught himself staring at Terrell and looked away before his best friend noticed. The sound of Terrell's lips smacking on the pastries made his stomach feel worse. Bile rose in his throat.

Enjoy your last meal.

A faint thump from a diseased heart pumped under the ground, playing an odd rhythm. His foot vibrated with the gas pedal.

Preparing himself, Dalton mentally checked off all the pain he'd suffered here: his wife's death rattle; finding his brother hanging from a noose; what Terrell did with his daughter. All of them paled in comparison to having a meeting with what he called home.

Terrell threw a half-eaten Boston cream on the floorboard, spilling its contents down his three chins. Drops stained his black hoodie. "Yo. I hate Boston creams. Know what I'm saying?"

"We'll pick up another box on the way home." The adult diaper under Dalton's pants rustled, reminding him of the mess coming. Seeing The Architect made his intestines grumble. Dalton clenched his butt cheeks together and hoped for the best.

He brought the car to a stop in front of the hollow, hands and legs trembling, despite the Xanax.

Terrell will wig the fuck out when he sees it.

Illuminated by the car's headlights, Terrell pointed to the opening of the forest. "Just what in sweet hell are we doing? Why is it so damn cold? This is Florida."

"You'll see." Dalton kept the headlights on and got out of the car. Snow cut through his suit and jacket, sticking to his face, his lips. Licking them, he tasted old loamy earth.

Dead leaves and twigs crunched under his feet like the bones of tiny animals as they approached the opening of the hollow. Dalton saw the red glow in the center of the hollow, shrouded in moonlight. "Come on, Terrell. Let's get this over with."

"I'm coming, I'm coming." Terrell wandered through the night's mist toward the opening of the hollow. "Man, I'd feel a lot better if you did this thing with me. We've been as thick as molasses pie since elementary school. Who's waiting for us?"

"You'll see."

"Fine. Won't ask anymore," Terrell said. All three of his chins swayed when he shook his head.

Dalton pointed to the hollow. "See the opening?"

Terrell squinted. "Yeah."

"Walk up to it, and when you see the fireflies, wait for *The Architect.*"

Terrell's eyebrows rose. He scratched his head. "The Architect? Why would someone call themselves—?"

"My good man, I can create anything," The Architect said through the thickest and oldest British accent Dalton had ever heard. "My masterpiece is almost done, my lads."

While clouds hid the moon, Dalton could barely make out The Architect waiting in darkness, so his memory filled in the rest. He looked as if he'd just finished a hard day on Wall Street, circa 1920, with mutton chops and a bowler hat to top it off. His body shook, as though he were warped celluloid played on a dusty, old projector.

Like each meeting, Dalton's left eye twitched, the migraine soon to come.

I can do this.

The Architect approached them, splitting the grass below his feet. Reality bowed, faintly shimmering around him. Something deep in the hollow had pressed Play, and all Dalton could see were those double pupils, rolling in their oily sockets. Tiny black rivers ran from the corners, tracing geometry across a face as pocked and scarred as the moon which kissed it.

Bringing his hands together in a steeple, The Architect stopped in front of Terrell. A switchblade smile cut his face, reminding Dalton of an artist's flip-book in motion. "What do we have here, my lad?"

Dalton cleared his throat, pushing the acid back down. "I—I need more time to find Harold's dad. While I'm searching," Dalton motioned to Terrell, "you've got him instead."

Terrell's jaw dropped. "The hell you doing, Dalton?"

"You disappoint me, Dalton Gladen, but let's see what you brought," The Architect said, approaching Terrell. "Come to me, my lad. Let's have a look at you." Three hundred pounds of Terrell rose from the ground, until he was nose to nose with The Architect. He grabbed him by the throat, lifting him higher into the air.

Kill him.

The forest's wildlife and insects fell silent. Dalton could only hear The Architect and Terrell.

Terrell's hands went to his neck as he choked. "It— it hurts. Stop. Please."

"It *hurts*?" The Architect cocked his head. "Pain is just one of my hobbies. A hobby the world will soon know."

The Architect placed his right thumb on Terrell's forehead, just above where his eyebrows met. "Your spine was crushed in two places. Your hips, shattered. A few years ago, yes?"

Terrell managed a nod.

Dalton tried to move, to breathe. Nothing.

The Architect licked his cracked lips. "Your nerves smell sweet, indeed." Small pieces of rusted barb wire grew over his teeth, splitting his cheeks. A few barbs stuck out from below his eyes, teasing the air as they grew toward Terrell's face.

"Dalton. Help," Terrell managed.

The Architect's fingers caressed Terrell's face, wiping away tears. "I know where every nerve in your body starts and ends. Those pathways," His barb wire maw spun in a circle, like heavy machinery, "they know so, so much."

God, I hate that sound.

Sparks flew as the barb wire smashed together, forming a sawblade that whirred to life, sending sleeping birds from their nests. Metal cutting metal echoed off the massive oaks and birches. The Architect's face split as the blade came out. Dalton strained to hear The Architect's words over the din.

"Whether they're in your spine, your teeth, your intestines—I will find each and every one of them. Once I string them around your spine, you will be my new cello." The Architect leaned in close to Terrell's ear, mouth whirring faster. Black oil splashed Terrell's face. "My lad, you will sing."

The Architect shoved a hand into Terrell's mouth, and Dalton tracked its progress on the way down, relishing every moment. "After I'm done playing you, I'll wipe that cesspool you call a mind, and you'll forget me, which is for the best, so that we may start again." He yanked a handful of fat from the depths of Terrell and flung it to the ground. A wet plop echoed through the hollow. Flies hummed. Steam rose from the pile, making Dalton retch.

Distress scrunched Terrell's face. His hand went to his chest.

"Not yet. That's too easy. Here, let me help," The Architect said, removing his hand. "Even better, my boy, I have another use for you in this game Dalton is playing." The Architect gazed at Dalton, his eyes a blur. Everything grew darker.

Dalton blinked and The Architect was mere feet from him, Terrell floating just behind.

With a flourish, The Architect released Dalton. He dropped to the ground, his hands breaking the fall.

"Where is Harold's father, Dalton Gladen?" The

Architect reached down, grabbing Dalton's chin and angling it up. "Your friend's father escaped us and is causing proper hell!" Each word sounded like silverware scraping a slate table; the barb wire began grinding together again.

The Architect leaned in close, until Dalton could smell the rotten things trapped in that hole which sucked the air from his lungs. Grabbing Dalton's head and angling it just right, he inched the saw's blade closer to the corner of his eye. The blades whined in protest.

Dalton blinked as black oil splattered his face. It smelled of burning tires. "I need a new grand piano. I miss hammering on nerves."

"No. I—I'm friends with his son—"

"You are not listening."

Dalton felt the grip on his skull tighten, pulling him closer toward a dim light flickering in The Architect's throat.

"I'll get him. Don't," Dalton said.

The Architect paused. "Are you certain? Would you like to see my garden? It's in bloom when the moon hits it just right."

"I don't *want* to see. Just give me time. Please."

"Remember *why* they call me The Architect, Dalton Gladen. I've made a god that slumbers under the very earth beneath us. I will wake it. You will serve it, my good man."

Rusted steel kissed the corner of Dalton's eyeball, sending a lightning bolt through his head, the spikes shredding and scooping it out. As the blade dug into the bone, Dalton's skull and jaws vibrated. Warm blood ran down his cheek, frozen by the time it reached his chin.

Fireworks went off in Dalton's head as he screamed his throat raw. He could feel his heartbeat in what was left of his eye and its socket. It beat in time to the infernal heartbeat of what The Architect was making beneath the ground.

The Architect let go of him, licking the barbs. Pulling a handkerchief from his pocket, he dabbed his brow. "Should you fail to bring him forth to us in three days, I will give your daughter a proper showing of my garden. Let her touch her grandfather's face as it blooms."

Dalton shook his head, instantly regretting it. A dull thud, like a clock, ticked the minutes he had left away inside a hollow eye socket.

The Architect pressed his fingers to Dalton's lips. "I will have the people of this town breaking that door of your precious mansion down, changed, and hungry for *you*. We need him back to us!"

With care, The Architect composed himself. He placed his gloved hands into his vest's pockets, hands that were capable of magic. Of anything. He straightened his tie, twitching and writhing with spiders. "Now, if you will excuse me, we both have a lot of work to do. You have letters to send to the people of Shady Hills. Divide and conquer is a good way to start. Should you fail, you will know my skills as a pianist, and so will your friend, Harold."

Another flash of his smile, and The Architect, along with Terrell, disappeared.

Dalton, finally, shit his pants.

Back at his BMW, Dalton slipped inside. The dome light dimmed like the fireflies that followed The Architect back into the hollow.

He texted his daughter, *I love you,* then shut his cell phone off.

At least she's out of state.

"Fuck it. Let Harold deal with it. He should have left me back in Iraq, anyway." After all, it was Harold's dad that escaped, not his.

Dalton pulled his Glock out of the glove compartment. He pulled the slide of it back, loading a round into the chamber. *I know if he can escape this shithole, I can, too.*

He stuffed the barrel into his mouth, and, once he pulled the trigger, exited this world the same way he came into it. In darkness.

CHAPTER 1

COVERED IN SWEAT from the nightmare, Harold rose out of bed, gasping for air. Like the doctor at the Veterans Affairs taught him, he scanned the room to bring him back to the familiar. Faint pinpricks moved up and down useless legs. It did little to help, much like the doctor's advice to write letters to the families of the fallen soldiers he had served with back in Iraq.

They're dead. Nothing I write can change that.

Popping some Xanax and shaking his head helped clear the illusion of sand, and the little girl he tried to save. He watched the ceiling fan—no, helicopter blades. Faintly, he could see her body jumping with each round that hit her.

Enough. You're home now. Get control of yourself, Marine.

Home. Smack dab in the armpit of America: Shady Hills, Florida. He lived in a double-wide that wasn't much to look at in a neighborhood that had seen better days. Even those who lived there weren't exactly the cream of the crop. Heroin and fentanyl flowed as freely as its rivers, depositing dirty needles and overdosed druggies on their banks.

As the past dissipated, he took in the nicotine-stained walls that boxed in his soiled mattress. A weathered chest of drawers, older than dirt, leaned against the wall, atop it the last family photo taken before his wife left him. Too much anger, too much silence, and, especially, too much alcohol.

That was a long time ago, but Harold and Time didn't get along so well. Every moment from Iraq etched lines across his permanently sunburned face; even now he could feel the memories infecting him. He stared at the picture of his son, Dale, waiting for it to center him.

"Dale?" Harold said, and stretched, taking in the pleasant smell of the oleanders that wafted through the crack in his window. It did little to soothe his shaking hands.

The sixteen-year-old showed up in the doorway, carrying a thick book on human biology. With his ex-wife's help, Harold hoped they could put him through medical school.

"Morning. Want some breakfast?"

Dale's hair hid his features; Harold could barely spy the grimace. Dale said something, too quiet to hear, but he knew it was directed at him.

His son just swayed where he stood, looking somewhat anxious. "Whatever will make the weekend pass faster so I can get back home to Mom."

Harold could feel the weathered fabric of his heart tearing.

I'm not that man anymore. When will he see that?

Angling his body toward the edge of the mattress, Harold pulled his wheelchair close.

Something is missing.

Looking down on the dirty floor, Harold saw his

life all at once: stubs from the disability checks, his little U.S. Marine Corps flag, empty bottles of booze. They served as a reminder of what would happen if he fell off the wagon.

Harold turned his attention back to Dale. After today, he'd be back with his mother. He hated those empty days when his thoughts were consumed with his boy.

God how I'll miss you.

Dale mumbled, "Let's just get it over with."

"Well, give me a second." Harold slid into the rusted wheelchair.

Ever since his mom talked to him about me, *it's like I don't know him anymore. What I did. Why we're not together.*

Harold mussed Dale's hair and he recoiled.

Don't go too fast.

Harold cleared his throat. "We're going to make the best waffles today. I found a new recipe on the Internet."

It's a wonder your mom lets me see you at all.

Again, Dale's sullen face was behind a curtain of bangs. "Yeah."

"Okay. Let's go make some waffles."

Maneuvering the wheelchair out of the bedroom and into the hall proved easier with coffee in his system. Without it, he did his best. By the time they made it into the hallway, a sharp pain shot up Harold's left side where the colostomy bag attached to his guts. Little drops of the contents leaked out the side, landing on the floor.

Not another infection.

"I have to go to the bathroom. Be right back."

"Fine," Dale said. He clutched the book harder, gripping the spine as though trying to break it.

Harold rolled as fast as he could down the hallway's warped linoleum floor. Holes in the walls from where he had put his fist through flanked him. Getting the wheelchair into the bathroom wasn't easy, the modest room being too small. The right wheel closed the door, while the left wheel got stuck between the toilet and rusted sink. The morning sun's rays illuminated a shower curtain covered in black mold.

"Son, I'm okay. Just stuck is all."

Dale started pounding on the door. "Now I have to babysit you? Christ, Dad. You're a mess."

The sound of his fists beating on the door let the bad memories reenter his mind. Instead of being in a bathroom, he was running for the Black Hawk, carrying that little girl, when the bullet hit his back.

"It's okay, Dale. Be out soon."

The bullet hit his back all over again, shattering his spine. He remembered wiggling his fingers, moving his head, trying to make his toes move too, as his fellow soldiers pulled him away. The crack of the insurgent's AK-47 killed them.

As they had dropped him, he'd chanced a look behind him, saw the girl missing the top of her head, and right then the madness took hold of him for good. He could only watch as her tiny body jumped as each bullet struck her.

Stop. It's just a flashback.

"Really?" Dale said. "Can you get anything right?" Now the beating was so strong and loud, he feared— and quietly hoped—Dale would break the door down. Then another boom came, and it wasn't on the bathroom door.

"Help! We need help," Harold said.

One last boom and he heard the rickety front door swing open and hit the wall. "Oh, what now?"

Outside the bathroom door, he could hear someone mumbling. "Where's your Pa?"

"In the bathroom, hillbilly," Dale said. "Do you know what a bathroom is, or do you just shit in a hole in your backyard?"

"That you, Tom?" Harold said.

"Shut up, boy," Tom said. "Been a crazy morning. Need to tell your son to shut up."

Tom managed to open the door about a foot, and then stopped when it banged against the wheelchair's worn and greasy wheel.

"You can't do shit to me, you old fuck," Dale said. "Just take it out on your wife, I mean, sister, when you get back to whatever squalor your kind lives in."

"I'm stuck. Christ's sake, help."

"Only if it'll get that faggot of yours to shut the fuck up, I'll help."

Oh, I'll deal with you after you get me out. Bet your ass, you son of a bitch.

Tom pushed the door the rest of the way open with his fingertips, as if it was so easy. Rolling back and forth on the balls of his feet, his face distressed, Dale stood there with his bangs back in his face.

Harold tried adjusting the wheelchair in the cramped space. "Hold the door for me, I think I can—"

Tom tossed the Sunday paper into his lap. Hard. Not that Harold could feel it. Only little pinpricks. He let his hands clench and unclench on the wheels. Despite being stuck in a wheelchair, all he'd have to do was get one hand on Tom, and his training would kick in.

Just breathe. Breathe.

It didn't work; every vein in his head thumped. Warmth spread over his left temple. A piston was knocking, about to blow.

"Tom, can you help me with this wheel? That's right, a little closer—"

"You ain't paying attention. Read the paper, damn it. You won't believe what's in there. And this ain't the first house I knocked on. Except for us, and for Danvers' family, everyone's gone. Poof! Like magic."

Something in Tom's eyes scared him. Cruel reminders of those dusty, feral faces. Most got sniped, or worse, an IED had hit them. He'd stopped learning their names, what was the point of that? Should they get froggy, though, he knew how to deal with them.

"We're going to talk about how you mouthed off to my boy."

Tom kneeled and pushed his face to Harold's. "Just read it, will ya?"

"The whole newspaper?"

Tom took a deep breath, closed his eyes, and ran his fingers through his hair. White flakes of dandruff landed on his Hank Williams Jr. T-shirt. Holes of various sizes pocked the front, full of chest hair. Apparently, Hank was singing "Harry Nipple".

"You're just as stupid as your son. No wonder you got shot. It's in the genes. Here." Tom picked up the newspaper from Harold's lap and opened it.

A letter fell out.

"The hell is that?" Harold said.

"You tell me." Tom picked it up, handed it to him.

Harold snatched the letter from Tom's hand and read.

To whom it may concern:

You're receiving this letter because in this little, hermetically sealed neighborhood, you have children. I love children. I love to play with them. Play with them in ways that give them a love you can't give them. As I'm peeling back their flesh—

"It goes on to say what this . . . molester—yeah, a fucking child molester—wants to do with your son, and my daughter! How he wants to kill them, and what he'll do after they're killed. Now, who owes who an apology? Huh? I want to hear it."

For the first time in five years, Harold wanted the bottle. Any bottle. Rum. Jack Daniel's. Harold's hand wiped at his mouth. "I don't know."

"Me? I've got my AR-15, so does Terrell. We've got ourselves something like a neighborhood watch group. We ain't gonna let this happen."

"Wait. What? How many people received these?"

"Everyone here in the neighborhood with children, I reckon," Tom said, nodding, eyes bugging out.

Harold folded the note. "What about the police? Have you called the Sheriff?"

Pacing the hallway, Tom chuckled. "You're three sheets to the wind, Hoss! This is real, and we gotta find who wrote these damn things."

"Let's calm down, okay? Let's see if we can't get Sheriff Lumpton out here. This is evidence. Maybe it has fingerprints on it."

Tom shook his head. "Didn't come here to give you the news, Harold." Tom sucked at his teeth. "Came here because, well, despite you being a cripple, you *were* in the military. We need someone who's run, oh what the hell you call 'em? Black Ops? Yeah, that's it. Police ain't gonna do shit. We both know *that.*"

I don't know what's worse, the letters, or him. "I still think we need to call the Sheriff," Harold said. "That's a lot of threats, which means we need—"

"Justice, my friend, is what we need. Real justice. You in?"

Harold placed his hands on the wheels and moved forward, but Tom just stood there, blocking his path.

Finally.

In a half-second, Harold reached out and grabbed Tom's belt buckle. He pulled him close until he could twist his arm behind him, bringing him down with effortless grace and ease. Harold wrenched the arm until he heard a pop.

"Aw! Fuck," Tom said, his face scrunched and flushed.

Fuck what the doctor said. Let. The. Monster. Out.

"Now you listen to me, shit for brains. Should you ever call my son any name other than his Christian one, I'll end you." Harold brought him closer and spoke loudly into Tom's ear. "Are we straight on that?"

"Yes! Let go."

Harold gave one last twist and released Tom.

"Dad," Dale said. Harold could barely hear him. He looked so anxious. "Are you trying to get arrested? Dumbass."

Harold's focus remained elsewhere, and he wheeled into the hallway. "Don't think you get a free pass because I'm in a wheelchair, and don't you bring this white-trash attitude back to my trailer again. Got it?"

If Tom had answered, Harold couldn't hear it. All he could hear was blood rushing and thudding inside his head as the piston knocked louder. Years of psychiatric treatment erased in mere moments.

I shouldn't have done that. Shit.

Still, Harold couldn't keep himself from making sure this never happened again. "Are we crystal?"

"Only crystal I see is the crystal in my watch, just tickin' the time away." Tom shrugged. "Maybe that tickin' I hear is for your boy. My daughter. I wouldn't want anything to happen to him or Jeanna-Lee. I come here and you're fuckin' useless." Tom hocked up a good one and spat on the floor. "Terrell and me are gonna handle this. Fuck your crippled ass."

Making a gun symbol with his hand, Tom let the hammer—his thumb—fall.

Tom stormed out. The front door banged against the siding, left ajar. In that moment, Harold stopped worrying about that little girl in Iraq. He needed to focus on whoever wrote the letters, and what he—or Tom—would do to his son, because Tom was right; he was disabled.

Dale cleared his throat. "I see the psychiatrist is really paying off. Nice. And on a fucking Saturday, too."

"Son? I'm sorry. I just—"

Dale scoffed. "Whatever you say. I just—I just want to get back home to Mom. Try not to fuck up again, okay?"

What fabric was left of his heart tore in two. Tom

and Dale were right. He was useless. Vomit raced up his throat as his body shook from the past's trauma. "That's not fair. You know it."

"What time is it?"

Looking at his watch, Harold noticed time had stopped. Flicking the hallway light revealed the light had burned out, too.

The heat from his nightmare and anger had worn off, replaced by a cold that reminded him of nights back in the desert.

"The power is out, Son, but it'll probably come on soon. It's gonna be okay."

Dale rolled his eyes. "Great. I've got that big biology exam coming up. You know that." Dale shrugged. "How am I supposed to study without my laptop?"

Harold thought for a moment. "It had full battery last night."

CHAPTER 2

HAROLD WHEELED HIMSELF into the small, bare living room. A moth-eaten couch and a La-Z-Boy took up most of the space. Newspapers and empty fast-food bags covered a glass table. Dale rocked back and forth in the corner. Harold rolled up to him.

"Do you need your meds early? Would that help? I can give you one of mine, if you—"

"No."

Seeing his own breath in the air, Harold wrapped two blankets around Dale, and one around him. He rubbed his arms until he stopped shaking.

"It's cold," Dale said. "It *never* gets this cold in Florida."

"I know, buddy. The power will be back on soon."

"Is *he* coming back?"

"Shh . . . " Harold massaged Dale's shoulders, ran his fingers through those beautiful, black locks. "Tom's gone. We're safe."

Dale recoiled from him. "Stop. Don't—just don't, okay?"

Harold sighed. "Okay."

The contents of the letter swirled in his head, reminding him of his limitations, of things he thought were long gone. There wasn't a drop of alcohol in the trailer, but that didn't stop him from wondering if his ex-wife might have missed one of his old stashes.

You're better than this. Call. The. Sheriff.

Harold pulled his cell phone out of his pocket and dialed 9-1-1. "We're just fine. Gonna call the Sheriff." The screen responded with the bane of modern society: No Service.

Mary's got a landline next door. The thought drove a frozen spike between his eyes. *She rejected you. Wanna drudge that up, too?* Harold rubbed legs that he couldn't feel and hoped one day he could be like them.

"Want to go see Mary?"

"I guess."

Rolling them to the front door took some effort, but he managed to open it. They went down the wooden ramp Mary had made for him. Dilapidated trailers dotted both sides of the streets, with palm and oak trees shading each one of them. Their paint had long faded away, leaving washed out pastels that looked like children's watercolors. Most lawns were so overgrown, Harold couldn't see the concrete blocks beneath the rusted and broken-down cars.

"Where is everybody?" Harold said.

A log at the bottom of the ramp stopped them. "What the hell?"

"What the hell, indeed," Tom said, smug. "Reckon we don't need your help, fucking cripple."

He came into view, Terrell behind him. Both had their AR-15s slung over their shoulders.

What the hell are they doing with AR-15s? I wouldn't trust them with water guns. Hell, I bought mine because it saved my ass back in the desert.

Terrell didn't look like himself. All the signs of meth-use were clear—battery acid face; thin frame; red, sunken eyes.

"Where you off to, huh?" Tom said.

Dale pulled in close against Harold's back. *Don't make me clean your clock in front of my son again.* "What is this, boys?"

Staring at his shoes, Tom snickered. "Figured we'd go see Britney Spears. We got extra tickets."

Dale crossed his arms. "Can't you get rid of these assholes?"

Harold pulled his cell phone out again. "I'll call the Sheriff and we'll sort this out. Believe me."

Terrell repositioned his AR. "Yo, man. Won't do no good. Every cell in the 'hood's down. Can't fucking hook up. Anybody seen Dalton? He and I need to talk." He scratched at the sores on his face, which seeped a gray fluid.

Tom spat on the ground. "Go suck a dick for that junk! Let *me* do the talking. Besides, no one has seen Dalton."

Hunkering down to Harold's level, Tom placed three more letters in his lap. "Whoever wrote these fucking things did it. We're cut off, dumbass. Look around."

Harold looked up and down the street, bereft of children and the neighbors mowing their unkempt lawns.

Fuck me running.

"Mary's got a landline next door." Harold motioned toward the log. "Mind moving this?"

With something familiar to Harold in his right hand, Tom inched closer to him. "Don't think we already tried that? Once you start acting like a soldier," Tom pulled the case open, taunting him with his own Purple Heart, "you'll get this back."

How in the fuck? That pain shot up Harold's side again, breaking his thought.

"You're shaking pretty bad, Harold," Tom said with a toothless smile. "Been drinkin' again?"

"Here's the bottle." Harold reached into his left side and flung his colostomy bag's contents all over Tom.

"Oh, sweet Jesus," Tom gagged. He made it to the edge of the ramp and vomited.

"Not cool, bro." Terrell managed, before he vomited, too.

Harold cackled. "You both better kill me or I'll shove that rifle up your ass."

Tom pulled his soiled T-shirt off and threw it on the ground. "We were just trying to get you motivated, you dick!"

Propping the AR against Harold's trailer, Terrell cleared his throat. "Yo. Look, we're not getting anywhere like this. He's not drunk, but you are, Tom. Stop talking shit."

Dale shifted behind Harold. "Dad, can we go? This is getting old."

Tom pulled the slide back on his AR and pointed it at Harold. "Don't you get it? Whoever wrote them letters could do this, and I'm damn sure whoever the hell it is has some fucking firepower." He puffed his chest out, giving Terrell a stupid grin. "Reckon we're gonna have to handle this ourselves."

A voice broke up the madness, and made Harold feel alive again. "Hell's bells. What on God's green earth?" Mary said, that sweet Tennessee voice distant as she approached them. "Harold, you and Dale okay?"

Thank God. Another Marine.

Harold felt like he was underwater. The deeper he swam, the darker it became. Memories of what could have been sharpened, then cut out, lost with the detritus of the wave.

"Harold, I can't. I just can't be with a man who . . ." she had said, motioning at his legs. "I want to have children. You understand, right?"

Shifting his wheels, Mary came into full view. She wore her best dress, the one she had made herself, with pastel flowers against a white background. Hair the color of wheat spilled down her shoulders, framing a movie star face. Fierce autumn eyes, eyes that Harold still dreamed of, scanned them.

This is what I get for serving my country. A constant reminder of what I can't have.

Tom pointed the barrel at her. "Hold up, little miss."

"Whoa," Mary said, putting her hands in front of her. "Y'all shouldn't be playin' with guns."

Tom's face flushed. "Look, it's G.I. Jane."

Oh shit.

"What did you call me, bitch?" Mary said as she moved closer to Tom. "Why don't you put that penis enlarger down and we'll find out who's a bitch? Wouldn't be the first time I kicked your ass, would it?"

Tom stared daggers at Mary, his face darkening red. "You call flying drones into terrorists, as opposed to being on the ground, the same thing? Did ya' enjoy playing video games?"

A laugh escaped her. "Unlike your wife, I'll put you

in the hospital. Right here. Right now. So go on, boy. You feel froggy, then jump.”

God, I love her.

“Oh, snap,” Terrell said.

“Shut up,” Tom said, and placed his AR-15 next to Terrell’s.

Mary smiled and crossed her arms. “That’s a damn sight better. Let me guess. This about those letters?”

“No.” Tom shook his head. “We’re all upset Brad Pitt and Angelina Jolie broke up. Got any tissues?”

Mary kept her composure. “Anybody got a phone that works?”

Shit.

Dale’s fingers squeezed Harold’s shoulders tighter. “You’re not listening.”

Harold refocused his thoughts, forgot he was the world’s biggest loser for a while. “Your phone don’t work at all, Mary?”

Mary shook her head. “Nope. Both my cell and cordless are as worthless as tits on a warthog.”

Dale’s head poked out to Harold’s side. “Hey, Mary.” His grip loosened just a bit.

“Hey, little buddy. You all right, sugar?” Mary said, approaching them.

Dale fumbled his fingers. “It’s cold, and I—”

Rounding the gravel street corner, Sheriff Lumpton’s Police cruiser came into view. It rolled quietly down the street. Mr. Danvers’ wife and son ran inside their trailer and slammed the door.

The rusted cruiser came to a stop down the hill, two trailers up from Harold’s. Sheriff Lumpton opened the car door and, with some effort, managed to get all three-hundred-pounds of him out of the cruiser. He pulled at his jeans, hiking them back up. "Finally. People. Glad to see ya', Harold. What's going on?"

Harold rolled closer to the end of the ramp. "Sheriff, you won't believe what's happened."

"Be surprised what I seen this morning. Knocked on a lot of doors on my way here, and you're the only people I've seen."

Harold handed the Sheriff one of the letters. Lumpton scanned it, sucked his teeth, and handed it back to him. "You got one too, huh?"

"Everyone with a kid," Harold said. "What are you going to do? How many units do you have out? Where is everybody?"

Lumpton hiked his pants up again. "We'll put a pin in that for now. Something else is going on that takes priority. That why ya'll got your rifles?"

Harold pointed at Tom and Terrell. "Yep."

Mary was so close Harold could smell the shampoo and conditioner she used. Placing her hands on her waist, she said, "Tom pointed his *penis enlarger* at us."

Harold and Dale laughed. He etched the memory in stone so he could savor it forever.

Shotgun in hand, the closer Lumpton approached, the worse he looked. His trademark mustache wasn't waxed but splayed, his clothing drenched in sweat.

Why does he have his shotgun?

Lumpton waddled to Harold's ramp, leaned down, and placed his hands on his knees. Each breath an asthmatic whine. "That true, boys?"

Tom began to whistle.

"That's a question." Lumpton composed himself and stood up. "Who should I start with? Hear no evil, speak no evil, or see no evil? We're in serious shit. None of this makes sense."

Terrell spoke first. "Yo. Tom said he knows who wrote the letters. He said we needed Harold's help. He's just fooling. Being a dick."

Tom shook his head, raising his hand. "Honest to God, Sheriff, that ain't what I did. We just came over—"

"To wish him happy birthday? Here." Lumpton picked up Harold's Purple Heart and handed it to him, before ruffling Dale's hair. "Now that's a damn sight better. You okay, Dale?"

"Just surrounded by assholes."

With a sigh, Tom kept his hands up. "We helped Harold, Sheriff. Got himself stuck in his bathroom."

Lumpton pushed his hat back on his head, wiping sweat from his brow. "That true, Harold?"

Fuck me. "It's true, but not five minutes later I come out with my son to see Mary and found this." He pointed to the massive log at the end of his ramp. "Tom pointed his gun at me. I'd like to file a report."

Mary walked to the ramp. "Me, too. Only *men* should carry rifles."

Dale stepped around Harold's wheelchair. "Fucking douchebags."

"Hey," Harold said. "Language."

"Sure," the Sheriff said, "only if we had computers that worked. Don't have the paperwork on me. Stupid car gave out as soon as I came into the neighborhood." Panting, he pointed up the road. "Thank God and Greyhound this road is a hill."

"What?" Mary said. "That even possible?"

Hearing the hurt in her voice gave Harold the shivers.

No power. No phone. Even cars won't work. And no one is home except for the Danvers.

Lumpton hiked his pants back up again. "Boys. You know how to work those rifles? I don't wanna get shot in the ass."

"Yes, sir," Tom said, and gave Harold a shit-eating grin.

Picking his AR-15 back up, Terrell pulled the slide back, loading a round in the chamber. "Man, I'm staying here with Harold. No offense, Tom, but you *were* being an asshole."

Harold beamed. "Thanks. I could use the help."

Lumpton pumped a shell into his shotgun. "Tom, I'm gonna need you to not shoot me in the back of the head with that thing, we understand each other?"

Mary approached the sheriff, hands up, as if to calm him. "What are we talking about here? Why's the power out? Why can't anyone make a phone call?"

Lumpton frowned. "Dalton's a Navy Seal. I know you don't like to hear that, Harold, but we gotta start somewhere. None of my deputies showed up for work today. If I were a gambler, which I'm not, just be clear about that, I'd say we're looking at a lot of bodies. This is a ghost town now. Everyone's car is in the driveway."

Dale stormed off inside the trailer, slamming the door behind him.

"There's no way. I mean—"

The sheriff looked away, pensive. "We'll do it by the book. I promise."

"Dalton's just a suspect, right, Sheriff?" Mary said.

"Sure." He turned to Tom. "Ready?"

"Yes, sir."

"Yo. If you can, Sheriff, bring Dalton back with ya'. I need to talk to him. It's really important."

The sheriff tipped his hat at Harold, with a nod. "We'll be back soon, Harold. Hold the fort."

Harold rolled to the end of the ramp, just before the log. "We need to talk, Mary. I need your help."

Mary looked at Harold's trailer, as if appraising it. "You want me to come inside?"

"Dale's a handful, thanks to all this bullshit. He needs all the help we can give him."

She nodded, walked up the ramp, and held the door open for Harold.

He stopped next to her. "I think I know what's behind this, and it's gonna make you laugh."

CHAPTER 3

HAROLD MANEUVERED HIMSELF into his trailer. "Make yourselves at home. Sorry it's not much to look at." Newspapers and ads from the mail littered the floor. Dusty family pictures hung loose on the cobwebbed walls.

"What is happening?" Mary said, rubbing her arms for warmth. Her flip-flops were sticky on the cracked linoleum floor. "I grew up in the Smoky Mountains, but I've never felt cold like this."

"Probably climate change," Harold said.

His face flushed when he saw her wrinkle her nose. "From now on, I'm cleaning your trailer." Mary pointed at the garbage bags stacked against the walls. "Don't recall you being a hoarder."

"Ha, ha," Harold said.

Dale rushed past him to the couch and lay down.

Terrell put out his cigarette in Harold's overfilled ashtray. "Yo. Mind if I crash, man? I haven't slept in days. If you see Dalton, let me know. Know what I'm saying?"

Harold locked his wheels. "Sure, but don't wake up Dale. May need to look after him, too."

Terrell shrugged. "Sure, man. Anything for you and your boy."

Patting Harold's shoulders, Mary leaned into him. "You're still shaking, sugar."

The piston started knocking again. "Was doing all right until Tom came by. He shouldn't have said what he did. What you did—?"

"Let's change the subject."

Smooth move.

"Don't worry about me," Mary said. "You okay?"

"I'll be better soon," Harold said, offering her a fake smile. "You?"

"Same."

Harold motioned toward the living room. Mary navigated her way through the trash-strewn hallway to the window and spread the blinds. "Jesus H. Christ. It's Saturday. Where's everybody?"

Harold rolled up to her, and after a long pause said, "Let's talk. Have a seat."

On her way to the La-Z-Boy, she placed the picture of them at the carnival face down.

Harold locked his wheels. "It's not a terrorist."

Moving the newspapers and used lotto tickets out of the chair, Mary sat down. The leather creaked as she got comfortable. "How do you know it ain't a terrorist?"

Harold rubbed his sun-faded goatee, teasing the hairs with the tips of his fingers. "Cars won't start. Lumpton's cruiser's from the 70s, which means there's no computer in it."

"My old generator is dead. Thing's been working for years. This morning?" Mary made a *pffft* sound.

Harold lit a cigarette, scratched his head. "I thought it was hackers, but how do you shut down cars that don't have computers in them?" He shrugged. "How do you make everyone disappear?"

Mary leaned forward, massaged her temples. "Cell phones *don't* work. Can't get a call for—"

"No, I mean they still turn on. An EMP would've killed them. They wouldn't even turn on if that were the case."

Harold's mind continued to spin around in laps, looking for something, anything. Especially any technology the military had that he encountered or knew about back in Iraq.

Nothing.

The snores from the couch comforted Harold, knowing Dale had finally settled. Fire shot up his side again, doubling him over. He pulled his shirt up and saw red lines in his flesh around the tube that entered his body.

Oh, this is bad.

"Still got any antibiotics left over, Mary?"

"No. That looks pretty bad," Mary said, wrapping a blanket around her.

Harold rubbed below his ribs where the colostomy bag was. "Damn thing flared up again." Harold took a deep breath, then exhaled. "Waited four hours at the VA yesterday. One guy was screaming so loud, I thought I'd lose it."

Mary's eyes welled. "I know. Been there, done that."

The piston had slowed, leaving a dull thud in his head.

"Went to get my insulin this morning. Car wouldn't start." She shrugged.

Harold lit another cigarette. "You got enough insulin in case we're in for the long haul?"

"Ummm." Mary thought hard. "I got some waffle mix and PB&J."

That wasn't even close to an answer.

"Thanks, but I really need to know how much of that insulin you got left," Harold said.

Mary pulled out a napkin, dabbed her eyes. "Enough to last 'til tomorrow morning. Don't' go worrying about me. You've got your son to worry about."

You don't know the half of it.

She gave him a smile that sent a tingle up his spine.

Harold took a deep pull from his Marlboro. "Good. The military will probably have everything back to normal by then. That secret base, not two miles from here, is to blame. Set my watch and warrant on it."

Mary flashed him a movie star's smile; a fake one. "Hopefully."

Harold took a long drag off his cigarette and put it out. "It's the only answer. Wouldn't be the first time the military pulled something like this."

Mary shook her head. "Seems like the whole place has gone sideways, especially Tom. Terrell looks like a zombie from *The Walking Dead.*"

"I heard that," Terrell said from the dining room. "I'm trying to get clean again. Give a brother a chance. Know what I'm saying?"

Mary stood and leaned against the wall of the double-wide. "I heard something last night. It was *loud.*"

Harold stroked his goatee again. "Well, now we're on to something. What did you hear?"

She bit her lower lip, scrunching her face. "Loud. Like someone playing a symphony right outside my window."

"Last night, around midnight?"

Mary nodded.

"The military runs drills all the time."

Mary paced the room. "What do we do? It's the middle of November."

Harold coughed. "You cool with waiting for the Sheriff to come back?"

"Of course, honeybunch. We'll pull through this."

Harold wheeled himself into the modest kitchen. Flies hummed and buzzed around the dirty dishes in the sink.

"The gas stove still works. We'll boil some water from my well."

For the first time today, a sincere smile graced Mary's features.

"One important thing." Mary walked over to the kitchen counter and picked up Harold's newspaper. A letter fell out. "The letters. Don't seem like something the military would do."

"You're right."

A car horn echoed off the homes and trailers outside.

Mary and Harold went to the front door. By the time they made it outside, Dalton's new, blue BMW had come to a stop in Harold's driveway. Terrell ran out and joined them, arms crossed.

The car is actually running. Dalton will sort this out.

The sun made long shadows out of the oaks and palm trees. A stiff breeze blew dead maple leaves down the empty street. The silence was deafening.

"Dalton," Harold said. "What the hell is—?"

Sheriff Lumpton emerged from the driver's seat, his shirt and hands scarlet. "Harold?"

"Sir?" Harold said.

Lumpton motioned for him. "I need you. *Now.*"

Tom got out of the car and walked over to an oak tree in Harold's yard, his face ashen.

"Can someone move that log for me?" Harold said, motioning toward the end of the ramp.

Mary grunted as she pushed the log into his front yard.

Harold pumped his wheels as hard as he could toward Dalton's car. The breeze picked up, and sand hit his face. He squinted against it. Despite the cold, it smelled like the desert. Harold placed his right hand over his left, but it didn't calm the shakes.

Sheriff Lumpton wiped his brow, leaving a trail of crimson. "We need to talk." The sheriff looked off into the distance. Without his hat's shade, Harold could see how gray his skin appeared. Large beads of sweat rolled down the man's face.

The sheriff's voice was low. "You won't believe me, but you're gonna have to. Prolly think I need to visit the funny farm after this. There's a fox in the henhouse. Understand?"

"No. Where's Dalton?" Harold said.

Terrell walked down the ramp. "Yo. Where the fuck is Dalton?"

Lumpton pulled off his snap-on tie, unbuttoned his shirt. "You sure you're ready, Harold?"

"I'm ready," Harold said, causing his heart to pound. Starting the piston in his head all over again.

"The only road out of here just *vanished*. It ain't there no more."

Mary walked up to them. "What are you saying?"

Sheriff Lumpton placed a stick of gum in his mouth.

"Sheriff?" Harold said.

"Yeah . . . it's—" The sheriff knelt before him, almost whispering. "We can't leave. There's a forest there now."

"You're not making any sense," Harold said. He could hear their voices echoing off the vacant trailers. "You okay, Sheriff?"

"We drove up West Street, heading for my office. I wanted to find out what was what." The Sheriff wiped his brow again. "There's no way out. I mean, the road opens into a fuckin' forest." He chuckled, eyes haunted.

Harold cleared his throat. "Whatever happened must be stressful. I know that. However—"

"I'll pick you up, put you in the only car that runs, and you'll see the same shit. Weren't fake either. We got out. Touched the trees. Grabbed and kicked the sand. We went there twice. *Twice*. Ask Tom."

"What about Dalton? Did you see him?"

Lumpton sighed, preparing himself. "Yeah. Over here."

Lumpton popped the trunk. "This ain't gonna be easy."

Inside the trunk, the body bag lay.

"Did you assholes shoot him?" Harold said.

"No. Calm down. Hell, you can check our weapons if you want."

Feeling himself going back down that elevator, Harold nodded.

Lumpton held his breath and unzipped the bag. Harold lost count how many times he'd heard that sound. An indelible marker, stained black, forever in his mind.

"It's Dalton, all right." Lumpton moved one side of the bag, displaying his crimson head. The top right hung down in jagged pieces, smeared gray by the contents. The smell turned Harold's gut. Glassy eyes stared upward, as cold as the frost crusting them.

I feel like the giving tree.

Harold shook his head, closed his eyes. "No. Oh, no. Not—not this, Sheriff. Oh, God."

He touched Dalton's arm and felt the cold, suppleness of the flesh.

You saved my ass, but I couldn't save yours.

The sheriff's hand moved onto his shoulder. "I—I don't know what to say, Harold. I am so damn sorry."

Shaking, Harold pulled a handkerchief from his pocket and buried his face in it. *I swear I'll fucking kill who did this.* Harold squeezed Dalton's hand one last time, and for a moment, a faint pulse thumped against his finger like a tiny drum.

Fireflies, much larger than they should be, had made a highway of Dalton's throat, swelling it with their passage. Even in the day, they glowed.

Fireflies don't—can't be out in the winter. They sure as hell don't glow in daylight.

One crawled out of where Dalton's brains used to be and landed on Harold's arm. He placed a hand over his mouth. "Ouch. Bastard bit me." Harold pulled his arm back, rubbing the wound. "Stung like a wasp."

"The hell is it?" Tom called from the crowd.

"Hang back, will ya?" The sheriff zipped the bag shut.

After hiking his pants up, Sheriff Lumpton addressed them. "Dalton Gladen took his own life last night." Lumpton stared at the ground, removed his hat. "He left a note."

Harold thought of his son, hopefully still asleep on the couch with Terrell keeping watch, but his mind stayed with the fireflies. He scratched the bite mark, and then it opened. Clear, rancid fluid wept down his arm.

Harold had seen flies, maggots, even a camel spider, crawl out of the worst places from his fallen brothers and sisters in arms. All of that paled in comparison to this.

"Harold," Lumpton said, shaking his shoulder.

Coming back to the present, Harold's mind whirled like the gears in a finely tuned watch.

"I felt it only fair, since you were his best friend," Lumpton held out the letter to him. Harold accepted it.

Harold,

I'm so very sorry for this, but you of all people will understand. Remember when we were cornered in that square, bullets ricocheting all over the place? You should have left me there, because everything that was there followed me home. I'm damaged goods, and every therapist I see tells me I'm a monster. Well, if I'm a monster, what the hell are those terrorists? I tried everything. Xanax, alcohol, Roxicodone. Mostly a mix of all three, and I can still hear the children cry. That scream, and that little boy, just gurgling. I know it was my bullet that hit his throat. It won't leave my mind as long as I live. I had to do this.

You've been a great friend, Harold, but I sure as hell wish you'd have left me to die, with my own blood soaking the sand. I deserve this. Maybe, one day, you'll understand. My advice? Should you meet a man with a British accent, get the boy and leave.

Hard times are coming.

Yours truly,
Dalton Gladen

He'd heard that boy, too, every waking moment. The strangest things could trigger memories. Sometimes it could be the water faucet, other times frying up some meat. In some way, it was *always* there. A part of him, like his skin.

"I need a moment," Harold said.

He felt a hand on his shoulder.

Mary knelt in front of him. "We need you. *I* need you."

Harold grabbed the wheels of his chair and raced for the ramp. Mary called after him, but he ignored her, wheeling himself back against the front door. Voices called for him outside, begging him to return, but the only one he heard was Dalton's back in that square in Iraq, telling him, *"No. Leave me here."* And the gurgling of that poor little boy Dalton accidentally shot in the throat.

There was another voice, too; one he didn't recognize.
British.

CHAPTER 4

THE SETTING SUN bled through molten pewter clouds on the horizon. As he sat in his front yard, a stiff breeze blew past Harold, caressing the eaves of the houses and trailers. The sound reminded him of babies crying. Dead oak leaves slapped his face, then spiraled to the ground. Autumn's crisp cinnamon filled his nostrils. He pulled his jacket shut, thinking of the sheriff asleep in his bedroom, and Terrell nestled up with Dale, looking after him. Mary had fallen asleep in the La-Z-Boy.

Harold had taken more Xanax than his regular dosage. Euphoria coursed through him, dulling everything except uncertainty and dread.

Gunfire from down the street sent birds from their nests. Harold tried to place where the shots were coming from. Candlelight from kitchens and living rooms made piss yellow squares here and there. Harold squinted against the wind, scanning the homes. He kept his grip on his AR-15 tight.

"Hey!" Harold yelled down the street. "Who's there?"

He'd spoken with Tom earlier, and he was happy he didn't lie. *"Yes, it was a real tree. Here's some bark I cut off. A whole damn forest."* Terrell had said, *"I don't know, man, but maybe let's stay here a while."* Harold knew the military was working with projectors, but they weren't capable of what Tom and the sheriff spoke of. Nothing was.

He realized his hands were shaking, rattling the AR-15. It came in a flash, that little girl again. The feel of her hand. The hope of saving her. "I've got you," he'd said. "My mommy is down—"

Stop it. Breathe. Like they showed you.

Harold closed his eyes and took deep breaths until the fireworks behind his eyes dimmed. His hands were steady again.

A sharp pain ran up his arm, bringing him back to the present. Harold had scratched the bite from that firefly so much it was now an open, running sore. No matter how much pressure he applied, or how many Band-Aids he used, the damn thing wouldn't quit running. It hummed, too, like a sweet vibration in his bones. He even felt it course down his legs, his feet. There was almost a rhythm to its saccharine buzzes.

A whistle carried above the wind, straining Harold's ears. He looked down the street, squinting for its source. Veins in his ears pulsed, and he winced as it grew in intensity.

Mr. Danvers' son came into view, riding his bike up the street, honking a broken horn. It reminded him of air-raid sirens. The sound faded as he peddled by.

"Hey! Where's your mom and pop?"

Dave stopped the bike. "They've changed. I will too pretty soon."

"The hell does that mean?"

Nothing.

This is the fucking Twilight Zone.

Appraising himself, Harold felt useless. He let his free hand caress the side of his wheelchair, his prison. Dalton was dead. The power was out; the neighborhood closed for business. If Harold learned anything in the military, it was: *"Coincidences don't exist."*

The whistle returned. It was *God Save the Queen*.

Every nerve in his ears twitched as if they were hit with a thousand volts, while ozone flooded his nostrils.

Harold glanced up and down the street, searching for the source. All he saw were the last vestiges of sun scattering the tree's shadows.

"Mr. Stoe, it is *sincerely* my pleasure," a man said. His voice sounded British and old.

"Who's that?" Harold said, training his AR-15 on the vague figure standing only ten feet in front of him. "How do you know my name?"

"Oh, that won't be needed. Let me introduce myself, Mr. Stoe." Clouds passed the moon, revealing a man dressed and groomed for an older century. A wiry mustache joined muttonchops across a hard, cold face. "We seem to have a mutual friend. A *dear* mutual friend."

The stranger approached Harold, extending his hand.

Harold flicked the safety off the AR. "Just who the sweet fuck are you?"

"Well, if you will allow me, my good sir," he said, all smiles, those gloved hands outstretched. "I am The Architect."

Every instinct inside Harold wanted to pull the trigger, but it was his intuition that stayed his hand. "You can stand *there*. Where did you come from?"

"Allow me to un-ring this bell. I am a friend of Dalton Gladen's. News came to me of his death."

"Dalton?"

Suspect number one, identified.

The stranger moved closer to him. "I have been informed that Dalton killed himself. Is this true?"

"How do you know that?"

"Dalton and I—" The Architect wrung his gloved hands together. "I was told you were a friend of his, like myself."

Harold lowered the barrel of the rifle.

He fidgeted in his wheelchair. "How do you know him?"

Still, all smiles. "He and I met some time ago. I'm afraid he's made a terrible mistake, Mr. Stoe. Here we are. Stuck in a rut." The Architect frowned, nodding.

Harold gripped the barrel of the AR-15 tighter. "What relationship did you have with Dalton?"

The Architect's eyes widened. "Allow me to explain the situation, lad."

"Please do," Harold said.

The Architect made a *tsk-tsk* sound with his teeth. "Dalton affiliated himself with a most unsavory council. He could no longer hold up his end of the bargain, I'm afraid."

Harold chuckled. "I know about his gambling problems. You're not going to shake me down."

The Architect popped his neck, his smile growing larger. "That is not why I'm here. We have business to discuss, and any business meeting begins with a handshake." The Architect's hand was still stretched out for Harold, but with great reluctance, Harold shook his hand. The grip was firm but hollow, as if writing things tumbled inside, making it look and feel like a hand.

"Good. Now we can begin." The Architect looked around, surveying the houses, the trailers. "Shady Hills. The time has come, my good man. Do you feel that?"

Even through his dead legs, he could feel a low thumping beat. His wheelchair rattled. Harold wasn't cold anymore.

"That, sir, is the *life* of Shady Hills. It will be my masterpiece. I've been working on it for some time. Soon it will wake. A god. Imagine that, Mr. Stoe."

I've fallen asleep. That's it. Just a bad dream.

The Architect brought his hands together in a steeple. "You are wide awake, Mr. Stoe. Mary's stuck in a rut, too."

Harold's mouth wouldn't shut, no matter how hard he tried. He found it hard to even breathe. "How can you read my mind?"

The Architect's dagger smile caused Harold's vision to wink in and out. On, off. On, off. He looked different when the moonlight caressed his flesh. Large fireflies crawled out of the corners of his mouth, moving up his face, burrowing under his eyelids. Their faint green glow beneath the flesh tracked their path down to his lip. Flies hummed.

I've taken too much Xanax. This can't be real.

The Architect's face strained. "There's no giving in, Mr. Stoe. Be a good lad and help me find what I need." He motioned with his hand, giving a half-smile. "I have my duties. I'll need people like yourself to help, of course." He pulled at his coat's lapels.

"Help what?"

The Architect's eyes began to spin. "Why, my masterpiece, of course. You'll see it soon. Dalton," he leaned forward and gripped Harold's shoulder, "will come to see you. That's why I'm here, lad."

I felt his pulse.

The Architect pointed his white-gloved finger at him. "Now it is you, Harold Stoe." His smile grew, cracking the flesh up to his ears. Fireflies flew out en masse, forming an illuminated veil about his face, his head. "Nothing, technically," The Architect shrugged, "dies in Shady Hills. The heart still ticks, but really slow. It's in your best interest to bring him and your father to me when they visit. Then I can finish my masterpiece. You don't want a war. Especially with what I have created. Do you understand? *I will only say it once.*"

Harold watched this odd man's pupils split, then begin to spin. He felt like the dentist had given him some anesthetizing gas. "You need my help? My dad?"

Why do I feel swimmy? This isn't my meds.

The Architect clapped his hands. "That's the spirit, Mr. Stoe. You will let me know if you see them, yes?"

"Dalton's dead. My dad's been dead for years."

Breathe soldier. Breathe.

"You have no choice in the matter." The Architect's pupils stopped spinning, and the dark centers grew into little volcanoes, blurring his face, like a Dali painting.

He leaned into Harold, whispered in his ear, "We'll chat more about it tomorrow. Around tea-time." Harold could see his double pupiled eyes begin to spin again as his thoughts grew foggier.

"You will wake, and you'll see that my intentions

are good. That's our pact." The Architect lifted his bowler hat and wiped at his brow. "You will have to be clever. Dalton and Tom are right. There *is* a pedophile amongst you. One of the men inside your house *is* the pedophile. There's still time to help your son, if you hurry." Harold felt a warm, genuine concern in him.

Remember, you're just dreaming, lad.

Harold bit the inside of his cheek, trying to wake up. "Hell's that supposed to mean?"

"It means that Dalton was close to figuring out who it was." The Architect stood, placed his gloved hands inside his vest's pocket again. "You simply must see my garden, but a few flowers have gone missing. The sound they make when they are in bloom is divine, Mr. Stoe." The Architect looked down at Harold's legs.

I'll wake up any minute, and it'll just be like any other day.

"My good man, when you wake—"

Harold could see rusted barb wire spread across The Architect's teeth, impaling a few fireflies.

"You will find yourself whole. You will have questions for the men you have given refuge to. We must start tomorrow. A new beginning for the world, Mr. Stoe. We begin this new age tomorrow."

"What will begin? What about Mary?"

Harold didn't think it possible, but that smile grew, and a plump, ghost-white tongue cleaned its rusted, gnarled teeth.

"We must see if you are worthy first. I think so. Do try not to let me down."

"Let you down?"

"Yes. Can you survive what this neighborhood

becomes tomorrow? After the good people of Shady Hills change into what they really are? I think so."

Harold opened his mouth, but he didn't know what to say.

"You need rest. We will meet again. Soon. Best of luck, old boy."

The Architect's features shook, then he faded away, like Harold's conscious. That night, he dreamed. For the first time since leaving Iraq, it was a different nightmare.

CHAPTER 5

Harold screamed when he awoke. Thankfully, the ceiling fan—no, helicopter blades—were turned off. Still, the vision of an endless desert was hard to shake off. Head pounding in rhythm to his boots on the sand. He sat up and reached for his pills.

What the hell?

Fully functional legs moved beneath his sheets. Sweaty sheets clung to them like that little girl did on that fateful day. He pulled the covers back, looking himself over. No colostomy bag, nor a scar from where it entered, either. An overall healthier feeling coursed through him. It was intoxicating. A soft euphoria as old dead parts of his body came back online. Firecrackers went off up and down his spine. Warm knitting feelings, with the natural need to—

Oh, shit literally.

The feeling on the toilet had an odd yet sweet release to it. For the first time in years, urine flowed from his penis and into the toilet. No catheter needed. It felt so foreign and hurt, but Harold smiled from ear to ear.

"Dale?" Harold grabbed the toilet paper and re-educated himself on its usage.

Nothing.

Shit. He sees me like this, how will he react? Better play it safe.

Harold went into his bedroom and sat in his wheelchair, the price for the ability to walk now apparent. No, "Oh, yeah. Just woke up and found myself fixed. Praise Jesus." Sticking to the status-quo dimmed the light of this bright, new beginning. Even the wheelchair felt colder. However long he was out, the temperature had dropped another ten degrees.

"Terrell?"

Again, nothing.

He washed his hands and the water chilled him to the bone. Shaking, he dried them off, then wheeled into the narrow hallway. "Mary?"

Judging by the sunlight on the floor it was midmorning.

All he found was a note.

Harold,

We're trying to get out. We'll come back for you.

—Sheriff Lumpton. Terrell. Mary.

Thinking back to the night before, Harold let out a nervous chuckle, all of it flowing like a movie on fast-forward. A shudder ran through him as he thought of The Architect, and what he told him. Harold slapped himself, waiting to wake up.

That British voice spoke in his head, "You are awake, my lad. My promise is good. Now let's begin."

"What are you doing, Son?" Harold said.

He saw Dale shift behind the couch.

"What's wrong, Dale?"

The more Harold wheeled toward him the more Dale crawled behind the couch.

Harold tested the waters and leaned forward a little, moving the couch away from the wall. Dale was curled into a ball, hugging himself.

"Everything's okay. Come on out, now. You need to take your meds."

"I don't want to talk to you. *Ever.*"

A tsunami hit him, and after the ocean receded and fell back, the darkness sucked the wind from his lungs, sprinkling ash across a sunset of new possibilities. Even the debris left their marks.

"Dale?"

The boy sighed, crawling out. Eyes glinted and flickered like fireflies. "I know what you did."

"What?"

"You punched Mom in the stomach when she was pregnant with me. That's why I have this . . . this . . . fucking nervous disorder! *He* showed me."

The second wave hit, bending his spine. Its dark gravity pinned him to the ground, carving furrows at his edges like the chalk lines of corpses. His corpse.

Harold snorted back tears. "That happened when I—"

"Stop." Dale raised his hand. "You hit her other times too, and you drank like Mr. Danvers said you did. Like a fish."

"What happened to *you*, Dale? Tell me."

Dale picked up a pillow from the sofa and threw it at Harold. "He told me everything! Made me sicker than Mom when she left. Ever since you came home, you've been a coward. You can't even write the families of those soldiers I hear you scream about in your dreams. You know why? You think it's your fault. It's just, it's just sad seeing you be the victim you are."

Harold raised his hands in surrender. "I was who I was. I've apologized for it, and I'll apologize again. Let's talk about you, and the *now*. Did someone try to touch you?"

"You're a one-way street, *Dad*. Always have been. Always will be."

In Harold's head, he watched—and felt—being knocked across the room by his father, just for wanting to hug him goodbye before he left for Vietnam.

I've never wanted a drink this bad.

"Everyone's changed. You think you're the only one?" Dale pointed to the window. "They *shamble*."

"Shamble?"

Dale looked like he was going to sneeze. He shook his head. "You heard me. Everyone. It's what they *really* are. That's what he told me. The British guy."

Harold got himself out of the wheelchair and walked to the living room window, pulled the curtains back. There was nothing but bushes, jasmine, and Mary's trailer.

"I don't see a thing, Dale. You sure you're okay?"

Dale was always full of surprises, good surprises, but never like this. It was like he was sick.

"I'm sorry for what happened. Truly, I am. I'm not that person anymore."

Dale pointed toward the wall, poking it for

emphasis. "You will be when you see *them*." Something large bumped into the trailer. Harold watched the dent form. It slid along the side of the trailer, bowing the wall in as it moved. The squeaking of its passage was deafening. Darkness filled the window.

Dale turned his back to him. "It's just survival now. Whatever keeps me alive."

Whatever was outside slammed into the trailer again, the indentation pushing the couch backward.

Dale moved the couch to the wall, shoring it back up. "Quick. Hide."

Harold watched as the darkness cleared the window, leaving behind a brown slick on the glass. He approached it, hoping to catch a glimpse of the aberration. Harold jumped backward as it hit even harder, stressing the thin steel of the trailer.

Time to do it. Semper Fi!

Harold patted Dale on the back. "I'm gonna get my AR-15. Best if you—"

A perfect circle of triangular teeth eased through the trailer's thin steel.

"Dale, come with me. *Now*."

Triangles spun, grating, like silverware stuffed into a garbage disposal.

As Harold let Dale tug him away, he caught a glimpse of what looked like the tip of a tentacle, circular rows of teeth seeking purchase.

Another bang hit the opposite side of the trailer.

Finally, instinct took over. An instinct he couldn't find back in that desert. Four good Marines were dead because of his inaction. Harold picked Dale up and ran into his bedroom, searching for his AR-15.

"We are *not* going down without a fight. I fucked that up once. Won't do it again." Harold found his weapon. He picked it up, pulled the slide back, loading a round into the chamber. "Move slow. We don't know what the *hell* that is."

"What if you shoot and the sound brings more of them here?"

Harold squinted, shook his head, trying to understand. "Them?"

Dale crossed his arms, turned his face away. "You weren't listening to me, were you? Typical. Welcome to my world."

"Calm down. Fear gets people killed, okay?"

"That's true," Dale said. "That could be the title of your autobiography. Just don't forget the word 'Victim' on the cover."

Harold motioned for Dale to move to the corner of the bedroom. "We'll go out the back window, head past Shady Hills, into the woods."

Dale's eyes grew wide, his mouth worked, but no words came out.

Harold hunkered down next to him. "What is it?"

"That's where the ocean is."

"A—A what?"

A familiar creak echoed down the hallway. *Creak-creak-creak.*

No. It can't be.

Harold started shaking again. A warm sensation ran down his leg, which, back then, meant ten hits from his father's belt, or punches. Depending on how drunk he was.

He picked Dale up again and pushed him in the closet. He cupped his hand to his son's ear. "Stay here.

I get hurt, run. Run like the devil. Out the window. Only if you have to."

Creak-creak-creak.

Dale's eyes welled with tears, his fingers ripping Harold's shirt.

Creak-creak-creak.

Keeping his body by the doorframe, Harold dared a glance down the hallway, and he saw it. Sunlight passed through its body as if passing through dust motes. It was sitting in an old wheelchair. A wasted, emaciated thing. Yellow skin pulled taut across bones. Tanks of oxygen hooked up on the back. A mask covered its shriveled face.

"Dad?" Harold said.

He's been dead for—

Every time he took a breath, the sound of bees in an empty soda can filled the space. Memories of childhood when he'd rather stay with the neighbors filled him.

"Look at me when I talk to you, boy." The belt would come down. Over, and over, again.

Harold smelled the Pall Malls, eliciting the worst memory of all: the night his dad smashed his mother's face with the telephone. Blood pooled from her head on the linoleum floor as she lay crooked. Her hand twitched, slapping the warm, wet tile. The sound was like jumping into a rain puddle.

"It's okay, baby. It's okay," she'd said before the seizure hit her. All the light had gone out of her eyes after.

His father kicked her in the stomach, doubling her spastic body into a fetal position. *"Get up."* Drunk on moonshine, he paced between them. *"I said, get the fuck up!"*

Ten-year-old Harold ran into their bedroom, grabbed the telephone, and dialed 911.

"I'm leaving you, you useless bitch. Try living and feeding that little faggot without me."

The front door had slammed shut.

"Help." His mother mumbled. Sounded more like, *"Hep."*

Harold ran to his mother and saw how half her face drooped down. It stayed that way, extinguishing a smile that could make the worst of his father's storms dissipate. Harold had someone to lean on, and, after she had made it out of the hospital, Harold happily nursed her back to health.

"Baby, I'm sorry, but you're the man of the house now. And I feel like such a burden on you . . . "

At night, engines like his father's '71 Nova would roar past their house, quickening his pulse. He'd sit on the front porch, waiting for his father to come home, and think long and hard about what he'd do if he did. After a few hours, he'd fall asleep caressing the .45.

Harold shook his head, bringing him back to the present.

His father slowly took off the mask, cigarette smoke wafting up from it.

His legs went weak for the first time since he regained movement in them. Harold placed his hand on the wall to steady himself. His vision was leaving him, along with the peace he thought he had made with his father's death. Jim Beam was calling. Telling him all the nice things he could do for him. Help him forget this was happening. He wiped at his mouth.

His father tilted his head to Harold, seeing the man that was once his dad. Before the emphysema claimed him. By the looks of it, he was close. "You listenin', boy?"

"What?"

"Ain't no one leaves *here*. Stop that line a' reasonin' right now," Harold's dad said, placing the mask back to his face, inhaling deeply. Harold watched his dead father's chest expand. "No one leaves. Never has. Never will."

A knock on the front door disrupted his father's image.

"Son, this is just like, 'Nam. Tunnels. Underground. They're everywhere. That's where Charlie's hidin'. Where The Architect is building something huge."

As Harold fainted, he heard that whistle again.

CHAPTER 6

$\mathbf{D}$*AD? GET UP.*
The words were slurred, underwater. White fireworks went off behind Harold's eyes. He didn't know how long he'd been out, lying on the floor. Cold from the linoleum floor numbed his body.

"Dad."

Bleary, Dale's face finally came into focus. Behind him, a harsh sun seared Harold's eyes. Squinting, the color bled through his hands, his fingers. *Just like that desert heat.*

"I'm up." Harold's sneaker's squeaked against the linoleum floor as he managed to stand. Teeth chattering, he rubbed his arms for warmth.

"You fell hard, Dad."

Harold brought a hand to his head, feeling the warmth and wetness. Using the breathing method brought the world back into focus, helped the pain recede a little. "Damn. What the hell happened?"

Dale turned from him, folding his arms. "We're dead."

"*Dead?* What do you mean?"

Pulling a curtain aside at the other end of the trailer, Dale pointed to what chewed up the trailer.

The sun kissed an endless ocean. Homes and

trailers replaced by a placid beach. On pin-pricked legs, Harold walked to the window. "What in God's name?"

"Yeah," Dale said, joining him by the window.

It looked like a hundred atomic bombs had gone off and paused, contained in perfect, translucent spheres. As its impossible shape moved, singeing the ocean and world around it, the globes containing myriad versions of annihilation formed crude legs and arms. A familiar heartbeat moved cloud and bird alike. Its sound passed through Harold, shaking his ribs, rattling his teeth. Sea and earth were gobbled up as it lumbered into the ocean, as graceful as a car accident. Patches of sand that turned to glass reflected pieces of the abomination.

The Architect's creation.

As it slowly vanished, so did its world. Homes and trailers of Shady Hills came back into view.

A knock at the front door made them both jump.

"Shit," Harold said. The pain returned to his head.

Dale ran in front of him, waving his arms. "No. It could be *him.*"

"It could be Mary, too."

Dale gritted his teeth. "How do you know it's Mary?"

Harold felt the buzz of fireflies course through his system, numbing things here and there. Reminding him of—

"*We have a meeting, Mr. Stoe.*"

The knock came again.

"Shit." Harold wiped his mouth again. "You hide in my bedroom. Go."

Dale ran into his bedroom.

Harold picked up the AR-15.

The doorknob twisted.

Harold placed his finger on the trigger, applying a little pressure. He pushed the butt of the AR-15 against his shoulder, took a deep breath, and waited. *Don't fuck this up.*

"Open up," Mary shouted, and Harold almost put a round through the door, and Mary.

"Point that thing somewhere else. Damn."

"Sorry. Can't be too careful."

Dale ran back into the room and hugged Mary.

"Hey, Dale. You feeling better?"

He gripped her tighter. "I am now. Not like dad is doing anything about how we're—"

"Dale. Cut your father some slack, okay? This whole attitude and outlook ain't gonna get you nowhere, sweetie. Your father's a—"

Dale stomped down the hallway and into his room. He slammed the door, then opened it, and slammed it again."

You're losing everything again. Where's a bottle when you need one? Just one sip. That's all. Just. One. Sip.

Harold wiped at his mouth again. "Been like this since he turned ten."

Mary hugged him. "Give him time. It's been hard on him. Been hard on you, too."

"Thanks. Where's everyone else?"

Mary cleared her throat, looked down at her shoes. "I don't know. We were out in the woods, and I went to pee and they got ahead of me. You wouldn't believe the rest. *I* don't believe the—"

"British guy. Calls himself The Architect?"

"That's him," Mary said, her eyes grew wide.

Harold rested the AR-15 against the wall, approaching her.

I want to hold you. Comfort you.

Mary backed away with her hands up. "What happened to you?"

"How much insulin do you have left, Mary?"

She looked away and smiled. "I knew it."

"Knew what?" Harold said.

Mary folded her arms, inhaled deeply. "He told me you'd be 'fixed'."

"Didn't really give me a choice. What do you think happened to Terrell? Lumpton?"

She motioned toward the La-Z-Boy. "Mind if I take a load off?"

Harold grimaced. "Take a load off."

"Thank you."

Mary sat down, fidgeting with torn pieces of her dress. She wasn't wearing her shoes, and her feet were caked with mud. "I—I don't know where they are."

"That makes two of us." Harold motioned toward the front door. "You've seen what's out there?"

Mary chuckled. "Kinda hard to miss."

"It's about Dalton. That British guy wants him for something."

"Dalton?"

"Yup," Harold said. "That British guy. Did he do anything to you? Hurt you?"

Mary nodded again, and Harold finally saw that low flame in her pupils. "He showed me pictures. Actual moving fucking pictures of this garden of his," Mary's voice broke. "I saw Mama. The cancer is still eating at her, even though we laid her to rest." Mary reached out and grabbed Harold's hand. "She's still there. In that *place*."

He brushed off used lottery tickets from the chair closest to Mary and sat down. "Well, that seals the deal."

"What do you mean?" Mary said.

"You said he has a garden, right?"

"Yeah."

"That's where we start. You with me?"

"Mama deserves it. *We* deserve it," Mary said.

"Okay. Then we'll start by—"

The voice was distant, more like the babbling of a brook. "You have no idea what you're up against."

Harold got up and pointed the AR-15 at him. "Terrell? Lumpton?"

It walked into the living room; head covered with a gore-streaked paper bag. Two holes were cut out for eyes. Dust motes floated through the body as if it were just a photographic negative, drained of color and life.

Mary shrieked.

"You should have left me back there, Harold," Dalton said, his head tipped to one side. "Then I'd be at peace."

Harold could feel Mary behind him, her breath hot on the back of his neck. He pointed the barrel at Dalton, despite an intuitive feeling that even bullets were useless. "I want—*we* want answers."

Dalton leaned against the wall. "You can't stop him. He's already got the both of you in his hands. You'll turn me in, won't you, Harold?"

"Only if it means ending this, yes."

Dalton chuckled. "And your father?"

"Sure."

Dalton nodded. "That's what he wants. You trust something that's turned everyone in Shady Hills into *those* things?"

Mary walked around Harold, toward Dalton. "What the *hell* is going on?"

Harold pointed the barrel at Dalton's head. "We want fucking answers. Now!"

"It's worse than hell. I should have never let him touch me. Like you, Mary, I did what I had to do to. My daughter was dying. Intestinal cancer. After the chemo did nothing, I didn't have a choice. He just showed up. After years of serving him, I thought I found a way out. Thank God Emily's out of state, and alive."

Harold laid the rifle on the table. "Then what do we do? You just said we can't—"

"*We* can't now, but soon. While he's weak." A nervous laugh escaped him. "They won't have a use for either of you, other than making you into instruments he can play to pass the time."

Mary reached for the paper bag atop Dalton's head, and he jerked back. "Don't touch me. You don't want to see."

Out of the corner of Harold's eye, he could barely make out Dale peeking from his door, watching, listening. "What is this *Architect* working on? Why does he want you and my dad?"

Dalton took a step back as if punched. He took a deep breath. "He's working on something big. Real big."

"I saw what I think you mean. The Architect—yeah, he showed it to me. Just a few minutes ago."

"What did it look like?" Dalton said.

"Like—it's indescribable." Harold shrugged. "Spheres with atomic explosions going off. All of them forming this, I don't know, body. It was huge. And whatever it touched died."

"I've seen those spheres before. He's using everyone who ever lived here to make something underneath Shady Hills wake up. He calls it a god. Somehow, he needs me and your dad to finish it."

Harold shook his head. "Why you and my dad?"

"And why us?" Mary said.

Dalton coughed into the bag. A crimson splotch formed. "Somehow, everyone still alive, present company, is needed for that *thing*."

"Think hard. Does he have a plan after he gets what he wants?" Harold said.

"Wiping everything out and ushering in a new age is what he said. This is not fun—" Dalton pointed at the bag. "You think I want to spend an eternity looking like this?"

Harold grinned. "You just want the easy way out, just like back in the desert. What can you say that'll convince us that we can trust you?"

"If I get out, we all get out. Understand?"

Harold massaged the spot between his eyes, trying to relieve the pain. "What's the plan, Dalton, huh?"

"I'll cause some kind of a ruckus and distract him. If not? He'll know you're there. Right next to where the hollow sits, that's where you'll find The Architect's workshop. He'll be busy, so we find your father before he can."

"After that?" Mary said.

"Once you get your dad and me, that's when we'll talk about our next move. Until then . . . "

Dalton vanished.

"Fuck," Harold said. "No way am I ever saying a word to my dad. Fuck that."

Mary wrung her hands together. "What other choice do we have? Sit here and wait? Starve to death?"

"You should have let me die with that boy."

"I only trust Dale and you," Harold said.

"It has my mama." Mary's face broke. "Has her in that garden of his. Please don't ask me to describe what's there."

Harold hugged her. "I won't. We'll start there."

He rubbed her back. "I just feel like I'm walking into a trap. Happened back in Iraq, so consider me an expert. Dalton's holding out for something."

Mary ruffled her dress. "It's better than doing nothing. So, let's do this. It's something, right?"

Harold closed his eyes, inhaled, and exhaled. "We'll have to be careful."

I can't lose you again.

"No shit. When?"

"Let me get my jacket and we'll go. You can wear one of mine."

Dale walked into the room. "You just gonna leave me here?"

"Yes. That way you're safe," Harold said.

Dale chuckled. "For once, you're making sense."

Mary walked up to him, ruffled his hair. "None of us want this, hon. You come along and that would be the end."

"Have fun playing soldier, Dad," Dale said.

Harold popped his neck. "Let's do this."

CHAPTER 7

HAROLD PEEKED OUT his window and saw the shambling things etch a darker pitch of black across the night. The wind blew so hard it was difficult to discern their shadows from the palm trees swaying about. A few of those things scrambled about, their features canvased by night. Not one candle burned in the trailers of Shady Hills. Harold turned off the light and waited for his eyes to focus.

"You ready, Mary?" Harold said.

She checked her shotgun, made sure she had extra rounds in her purse. "Yep."

Cold sweat beaded down Harold's face. His hands were so sweaty he almost lost his grip on the AR-15. As his eyes darted around, he couldn't help anticipating the crack of an AK-47, his old nemesis.

Mary cupped a hand to his ear and whispered, "You okay, sweetie? You're shaking again."

"Best I can be."

For the tenth time in his life, Harold held a flashback at bay. As his eyes began to adjust to the darkness, the trailers resembled stone houses and buildings. Every hair on his body stood up straight. Not from the cold, but what he didn't know was hiding there.

Stop. This is not the time.

Harold pulled Mary close. "Stay behind me when I open the door, and when we get outside, you go to my right."

"Okay."

Harold took a deep breath, then opened his door a little.

"How many?" Mary said.

"I don't see anything."

Harold could hear Mary's gulp.

He opened his door fully and walked down the ramp, Mary behind him, sparse moonlight illuminating the way. He scanned to the left, then to the right.

They're too dark to see.

A board creaked, echoing up and down the dark, silent street. Out of habit, Harold raised his hand and made a fist, which meant: STOP. Narrowing his eyes, he scanned their surroundings again, looking for anything out of place. The trailers and big oaks obscured his line of sight, though. So many enemies could hide behind those homes. Even their breath gave away their position.

Harold's fist became a hand, waving forward. Slowly, they made their way down the ramp. Frozen grass broke under his boots like fine china.

Carefully, they moved past Harold's trailer.

A wet slap hit the back of Mary's trailer. He grabbed her and moved them to the front, under the windows. "Crouch down, business end forward," Harold whispered.

The trailer moved an inch, the steel whining and scraping in protest. One by one, the boards supporting it snapped. Cinder blocks exploded, lowering the trailer about three feet. Then the side moved.

Now, my lad, prove yourself.

Harold stood and pointed toward the other end of the trailer. "Go for it."

Mary shook her head.

Oh, not now. Harold grabbed her shoulder, pulled her up. Mary made a run for it, and he tried to keep up with her.

The sound of metal bending and crunching split the night, silencing crickets and cicadas. Harold felt something warm and wet hit the back of his neck. "Run," he whispered.

Mary ran behind Mr. Danvers' trailer, and Harold ran behind his. He allowed himself a peek once he rounded the corner.

A black shape squirmed Harold's way like a massive worm, grass and dirt lost inside its bulk. Darker than any shadow he'd ever seen, the thing dwarfed the trailer behind him, blotting out the moon as it charged. He pointed the barrel at its core and took aim.

It stopped mere feet in front of him, revealing countless rows of teeth, spinning round and round, lit up by fireflies. Harold gagged at the smell of dead fish and salty ocean. Its mouth opened wider, and Harold placed his finger on the trigger, waiting for a nice round to go down its gullet. Then he saw a face on the tip of its tongue.

"Harold?" Tom managed.

Harold's jaw dropped. "Tom—"

Tom's body came forward, every inch of flesh sewn into a bulbous white tongue. Nerves attached to every orifice. Eaten up by the parasite's appetite. Tom shook with the frailty of a cherry blossom in a stiff breeze. "Harold? Help," he managed.

Bad memories came back. The worst. Unable to save the kid. Unable to save his entire squad; his brothers and sisters in the helicopter.

Same shit, different day.

Harold's finger tightened on the trigger. The report of his own weapon shocked him, making him jump and fire another round. He took aim as it reared back, wailing.

The head. Where's his head?

Harold's third shot hit Tom's skull.

The beast crashed to the ground, entrails and Tom spilled from its stomach. Despite the steam rising from the dead body, Harold emptied a full magazine into it. No real aim in mind, and when he heard the *click-click-click* of an empty mag, he kept pulling the trigger anyway.

"Harold," Mary called, running toward him.

He felt her hand on his shoulder, melting away some of the ice—both outside, and inside. "I'm sorry. I—"

Mary slapped him. "Not now, Harold."

Harold squeezed his eyes shut until they hurt, waiting for the sound of helicopter blades to stop. *They're not real. They're not real.*

He opened his eyes. "Thanks."

Mary looked over his shoulder.

"What is it?" Harold whispered.

She crouched down, pushing him aside. While Harold turned, he saw another one crawling in the street, headed right for them.

Finally, his instincts kicked in. "Let's go behind the trailers, into the woods," he whispered. "Is that close enough to that thing's garden?"

She nodded and motioned for him to follow. Harold dumped the empty magazine and loaded another, pulled the slide back.

Slowly, with boots crunching on frozen grass, they made their way to the end of the neighborhood, where the forest started. Mary stopped.

"What's up?" Harold said.

Mary met his gaze and shook her head. "Dalton's not helping. That's obvious. This—this could be suicide, Harold."

He crouched down with her, getting in close so as to not be heard by what stalked the night. "Then we'll just canvas it. Look around. Play it safe."

Mary's eyes grew. "Oh. Play it safe?"

"Do we have a choice? Besides, if he wanted us dead, we'd be dead," Harold said.

"If he's got Dalton, what use does he have for us?"

"My father. That's what he wants. It's like . . . " Harold said.

"Like what?"

Harold cleared his throat. "Never mind. We'll just play it safe. Stay on the outside and have a look around."

"We'll regret it if—"

"I know all about regrets, Mary. It's time I did something right. Not just for me, but the innocents in this. Tom has a daughter. There are other kids, too."

"Speaking of regrets," she took a deep breath and exhaled. "Harold, I told you I didn't want to be with you because you couldn't have children. That ain't the whole truth. I guess you saw the same thing I did. Only difference? I got to see the children on the screen, like some kinda computer game. I can't even touch a computer or a smartphone since. I'm sorry." Tears glimmered in her eyes, rolling onto her cheeks.

"Shh," Harold said and embraced her. They both wept. After a few minutes, he stood and started walking toward the mouth of the forest. "Only one way to find out what's out there."

"I know where it is. Follow me," Mary said.

Harold placed a hand on her shoulder as she nodded and pointed the way.

***

Once the fireflies came, outlining the entrance to the hollow, Harold brought them to a stop. "That it?"

"No," Mary said, pointing to a circle off to the right, where the brightest moonlight Harold had ever seen scorched the earth below it. He looked up at the white, circular column, where hungry tendrils sucked at the moonlight above, feeding, growing.

From a distance, a broken violin invaded Harold's ears, reverberating every bone in his body. He shuddered. "Fuck."

Mary pulled Harold's jacket closed. "I know."

He sat down, cross-legged, ran dirty hands through his hair. "You hear that?"

"It hurts like hell," Mary said, joining him.

"He's close."

"We'll have to be quiet," she said.

"Where do you think he's at?"

Probably everywhere.

Mary looked around in thoughtful contemplation. "Hmmm."

Harold pointed toward the garden. "You tend a garden, right? My money's on the garden."

"Mine, too."

"That music is far off, so we're going where he works. It's the hollow. If he isn't there, we'll get some good intel. A good old-fashioned reconnaissance mission."

Mary shouldered the shotgun. "Let's move."

They got up and headed toward the hollow. Harold almost fell.

"I hate fucking tall grass."

"You okay, hon?"

"Will be once we get there," he mumbled. The fireflies swarmed around the hollow, making it look like a mirage. Harold motioned toward the hollow, then the ground. "The closer we get, the worse the incline is. May need a ladder when we get there."

"Maybe try the circle?" Mary said.

"I bet that isn't what it appears to be either."

Harold wiped his brow. "As long as the music is far off, we should be okay."

As they moved closer, Harold got a better look. A jaundiced light burned inside the hollow, made of countless buzzing fireflies. Scarlet raged like a rash from its center, teasing the wind. Harold stopped. "Sure you still want to do this?"

"It's got Mama in there. I can't leave her like that."

Harold thought long and hard. Half his brain reminded him of his son, the other half was drunk with atonement for the past. That little girl. Not seeing the insurgent. Four Marines dead. Like a record player stuck playing on a warped vinyl.

"Mary, if we make it through this alive—"

Mary kissed him. Her lips were heaven, sending warmth down his spine. "Yes." She bit her lower lip. "Let's move, soldier boy."

Harold etched the moment in his mind, in every shade of color. His body floating away like a balloon.

"You coming?" Mary said.

Harold followed as a low thump made his feet itch.

CHAPTER 8

TALL GRASS GAVE way to hard clay, carpeted with the forest's detritus. Boughs of ancient oaks hid the moon above them. Sticks and moss crunched under their feet, echoing back to them from inside the hollow. Harold bumped Mary's arm and cocked his head. "We'll go in on the side, flank it."

Mary exhaled, her chapped lips making a *pffffttt* noise. "Better than just walking in and saying, 'Hey, ya'll. Thought we'd stop on by.'"

"Yep."

Harold walked toward the side of the path, ten yards from the hollow's entrance.

Fireflies darted through branches above the hollow, their trails a splash of autumn against the gray of November. Scarlet threaded through the insects, like a network of veins. That's when they heard the scream.

Harold covered his ears. "Stop. Oh, God. Stop."

Mechanical laughter bounced off trees.

Mary grabbed Harold's shoulder, turning him toward her. "That's her. That's Mama." She let go of him and ran toward the voice, shotgun in hand.

"Wait." Harold held her arm, pulling her to a halt, her face awash in the fireflies' pastel colors. "We go slow, like we said. Okay?"

Swatting at Harold, Mary pulled her arm away. "Fine. Let go."

They both came to a stop before the large, rusted door. Under it, crimson bled into the wind, floating like blood in a pool. A small square of steel recessed in its center.

"Fuck me," Harold slapped his face, preparing himself. "I guess this is it."

He looked at Mary and saw the same look he'd seen on the faces of countless soldiers, right before breaching a door.

The first snow fell upon his shoulders, carried by gale-force winds. Harold's teeth began to chatter.

A scream echoed up and down the hollow.

Mary slapped the door. "Mama. I'm here!"

Harold approached her, placed his arm around her. "Mary—"

She bucked out, pointed the shotgun at the door.

"No," he said.

"I'm coming, Mama," Mary said, barely audible over the wind.

Harold didn't have time to plug his ears. For the first time in his life, he was happy most of the damage was done back in the desert. An air-raid siren wailed in his head.

"Dead end," Harold said.

Creak-creak-creak. Creak-creak-creak.

Harold couldn't turn around. It wasn't the weather anymore. Memories of childhood when he'd rather stay with the neighbors filled him. Even in the wheelchair his father always found a way to reach him. One day a belt, another day an ashtray. The wounds felt fresh.

"Harold?" Mary came into focus.

"Yeah?"

Creak-creak-creak.

She slapped his face. "Wake up, please."

"Don't you hear that?"

Harold turned and Mary screamed at the thing in the wheelchair. Yellowed flesh pulled taut across the bones. Sprigs of hair swayed atop his liver-spotted head. Smoke drifted from his oxygen mask as he pulled it off, snapping the rubber that secured it.

His father inhaled, the sound of rain hitting wet gravel.

Mary pointed the shotgun at his father.

"Guns won't work, darlin'," Harold's father, Oliver, said. He pulled the face mask, billowing smoke, to his mouth and breathed deeply. "You're not supposed to be here, the both of ya'."

"*You're* not supposed to be here, *Oliver,*" Harold said. "You working for him? For that *thing* in there?"

Harold's father sneered, coughed up a wad of bloody phlegm and spit it out. "You move forward with this, Son, you'll regret it for all your days. They'll be long. Trust that."

Hearing that buzzy voice opened the deepest wound. "Back when I was only ten, after you beat the hell out of me with your belt, screaming, 'Look at me, little faggot', I watched you *bash* mom's face in with the telephone." Harold's body shook like a willow in the wind and wept as graceful as its name. "Fuck off so we can handle this, and hopefully," his fingers massaged the rifle, "you'll die with him."

Mary bumped into Harold. "I don't like this."

"Hear that, Oliver? Time for you to leave." Harold

pointed back the way they came. "You're still good at leaving, right?"

Oliver slammed his twig-like hands down on the arms of his wheelchair. "He. Wants. This. To. Happen."

Mary scoffed. "Really? I don't see you doing a goddamned thing. You're just making trouble."

Harold cracked his neck as if preparing for a brawl and secretly hoped for one. "You left me when I was just a child. The only thing worse? After you bashed mom's face in, you . . . " Harold looked at his shoes, massaged his temples. "You fucked up mom's face for good, you asshole. You took the only thing in my life that made everything better: her smile. I saw the light go out of her eyes!" Harold loaded a round into the chamber, pointed the barrel at his chest, "While she was down, you kicked her in the stomach. She had a *fucking* seizure!"

Harold's trigger-finger quivered.

"I made up for it, Boy," Oliver said, crossing his arms. "Got on the wagon, paid for all of it, and your mother forgave me. You didn't even show up to her funeral because I paid for it. You only remember the bad times. Can't say I blame you. Now is not the time to—"

The metal door shrieked, startling them.

Here we go.

Harold and Mary turned and pointed their guns at the door as it slid open. The grating shredded Harold's ears. Bright, autumnal light spilled out. He shut his eyes, turned his face. He could smell oil and machinery, like a busted motor.

The Architect stepped out.

"Evening, my lady, Harold. *Oliver.*" The Architect stretched his arms out as if to hug them all at once. "Come here, bloke. *Oh, how I've missed you.* Can't create a god without a heart. And yours is the darkest I've ever seen." The Architect grinned, licked his lips.

"Finally," Harold said, "one thing we agree upon. Have fun, Oliver."

Creak-creak-creak. Creak-creak-creak.

Oliver stopped beside Harold. "If this is what you want," scratching the side of his head—his tell that he was actually telling the truth, "you're worse off than I am."

Creak-creak-creak. Creak-creak-creak.

The Architect shrugged. "I must say, Harold, I am very pleased. Well done, Sir. Well done, indeed. You as well, Mary. You're both very good soldiers. I'll need that."

Harold summoned what courage he had, and placed his hand on his father's cold, wet shoulder. "If you're religious," he sighted the barrel between The Architect's eyes, "you might want to start praying."

"Pfft . . . " The Architect's body shuddered, a gray negative skipping against the vibrancy. "Bullets only go through me, lad. Mary's mother, on the other hand, is a different matter."

The Architect flicked a switch, illuminating his workshop. A thick wooden table was in the center, surrounded by those little spheres of annihilation. Tools and weapons hung from nails on the walls, swaying with the winter's breeze. Dead bodies, half flesh, half machine, rested against its walls. The smell brought bile up Harold's throat.

"Mama?" Mary said.

God, we're out of our league.

The Architect grabbed the wheelchair's handles and pushed Oliver into the lair.

"Baby? Is that you? Come let Mama feel your skin."

The Architect reached and pulled a string, illuminating the atomic parade before them. Encased inside perfect, translucent spheres, after-winds blew, dropping mushroom cloud ashes. And there Mary's mother lay, bolted to the table in the center, as The Architect worked on her body.

Staring at the sight before him, Harold could hear his heartbeat, feel the power go out of his legs. Mary's mother was carved into thin, vertical layers. Nerves suckled greedily into the spheres. "Is that you, baby doll? Mama has some milk."

Mary gasped, the color leaving her face, her arms cold in Harold's hands.

The Architect cleared his throat. "Come on in. You wanted to see, and lads and lasses, you will see, indeed." He took a sphere that had not detonated yet and placed it atop Oliver's head. "This will only take but a few moments, Oliver."

The Architect's eyes found Harold's. "Only one left for you to bring to me so that my masterpiece will be finished."

Mary lurched past Harold, leaned against the wall, her hand covering her pale face. "What—what have they done to you, Mama?"

The Architect regarded her as if she had asked why the sun rose every morning. "Why, it's," he flourished. "the beginning of a new age, of course." He bowed. "You're welcome."

Your only option is out-smarting him. Remember your training.

"What the hell do you mean, you sick fuck?" Harold said.

The Architect's eyes became furnaces. "Would you save your son or leave him to die? Hmmm?"

"Save him from what?"

Fireflies buzzed around and fretted about The Architect's face. "I held my daughters in my arms and watched them die. Right here!" He pointed to the ground and sat on it, rubbed at the dirt with his gloved hands. "I came to help The North fight The South. They ambushed us, and my daughters and I lost the path. I watched them die. Then, my own lifeblood drained out of me, and I was glad to follow them." The Architect nodded, smiled, then stood. He approached Mary's mother.

"Then I heard this rhythm, this heartbeat, and it showed me they didn't have to die, that no one has to suffer. All it would need was to be built. I have almost finished." The Architect spat out, slamming his fist through the table. Thin layers of Mary's mother shook. "I have saved your mother, given her a chance again, like the both of you!"

The Architect pointed at them, "You're ungrateful. Very obtuse. It's bollocks bringing arms here. Someone may get hurt."

Fuck you too, buddy.

Harold lowered his gun. "What are you going to do with this masterpiece of yours?"

The thing laughed. "History repeats itself," he began counting his fingers. "Oh, I have seen war. Before the ambush, my daughters and I watched General Sherman enact, for the first *glorious* time, Scorched. Earth. Policy. Oh, the South did howl. I can still hear the children's screams as Sherman's troops burned them alive." The Architect smiled at Mary. "Just like the children's screams you hear. But you were far away, off the battlefield. You lack perspective. Sherman was a genius, and so am I. It will work again. I was human then. I understood the division. But here we are, and history must correct itself before you tear yourselves apart."

"You don't know that. And you have no idea what I've been through," Mary said.

"She's right," Harold said.

The Architect placed his hand on Harold's shoulder. He could feel it flickering, like a VHS tape skipping. Shaky.

"I fixed you. To show that I'm a good sport, I fixed your son, as well."

The Architect's eyes expanded, began to roll. "I didn't *have* to help any of you. Why, I could just entertain my daughters with all the instruments I've made." That switchblade smile split his face. More fireflies crawled and tumbled out. "Oi," The Architect said, the sound scraping Harold's eardrums. "Be grateful and leave. What can you do? *Bring Dalton to me and leave me to my work.*"

The world went black.

CHAPTER 9

"**Y**O. WAKEY-WAKEY. Eggs and bakey," Terrell said.

The voice was far off, and Harold did his best to shake the grogginess away. Slowly, his living room came into focus. The couch was overturned, his La-Z-Boy was on its side. Harold tried to get up, but the pressure from his wrists and ankles kept him tied to the chair. Terrell loomed above Mary.

"Harold? Help," Mary said.

Terrell held a drill, which had a faint gold and red aura. Its bit pressed into Mary's knee.

"I wouldn't move," Terrel said, "this one is special. Stole it from that fucker while you all distracted him." He laughed. "He has so many. Made it hard to choose." Terrell looked it over. "I think I made the right choice."

"Stop this right now, Terrell," Harold said, struggling with his restraints. His heartbeat was on over-drive, signaling a migraine was on the way. He closed his eyes and saw the desert, felt its coarseness against his cheek. As two Marines ran for him, he realized he couldn't move.

You're not there. You're here. Breathe.

Terrell regarded him. "I want answers."

Mary's thin body struggled against the ropes

binding her to the chair, cutting little red circles on her wrists, ankles, and neck.

"Shhh," Terrell said, placing a finger over his lips. "It will only hurt once I drill *through* the nerve."

Placing his hand on her forehead, Terrell brought the drill-bit close to her eye, setting the tip just below her eyelid. "I'm not a fucking *pedophile!*"

Again, Harold tested the ropes that held him. Nothing. "Stop! Whatever it is, just fucking stop. Terrell, you know me, right? Let's talk this out."

Terrell frowned, walked over to Harold and sat close to him. "Talk about what? Talk about how Dalton just sacrificed me to The Architect and made me what I am now? Back on the meth, a meth that's singed my fucking lips. I know he's not done with me. He's using the both of you. What's his game, yo?"

"I don't—I didn't—" Harold managed.

"You're gonna sell me out to him," Terrell said, sucking at his teeth.

Terrell's finger pulled the trigger. "Just tell me where Dalton is, or I'll go to work on your boy. Like that thing did to me."

Harold pushed his head back as far as it would go. He could feel the vibration in his cheek as the drill-bit approached his eye.

Terrell let off the drill's trigger. "Where is he?"

"He was here," Harold said.

"When?"

"Just before we left to end that, that thing that calls itself The Architect. Dalton's helping us. I don't know what you're talking about."

Terrell turned on the lamp, inched closer to him. "*Helping* you? Word?"

"We made a plan, Dalton said he would help, and then Mary and I went—"

"That thing is still alive. Did he really help you? Choose your words carefully. Remember your son. Your precious," Terrell pushed the drill-bit into his chest, "fucking son."

What did Dalton do?

"Then let us help you. Hell, I want to figure this out, too," Harold said. "That thing in the hollow can't be trusted. Are you sure Dalton's to blame?"

A low growl, like that of a dog, came from Terrell's throat. "You always thought I'm stupid. Did back in high school, and apparently now." Terrell played with the drill. He exhaled, placed the tip of the drill-bit between Harold's eyes.

Harold felt the warmth as Terrell massaged the tip into his forehead.

"There, that's better. Where. Is. He? This happens to your son. Know what I'm sayin'?"

"He said—" Harold managed through ragged breaths.

Terrell squeezed the drill's trigger, on and off. On and off. "I'm more interested in where he is now. Last chance. This could get really ugly, man."

"He comes and goes as he pleases. He's helping us right now if you'd—"

"Not what I wanted to hear," Terrell said pressing the bit in deeper.

"He's right, Terrell," Mary said. "Untie us, so we can work this out."

Terrell smiled. "Then we'll all sit around and bake cookies?" Terrell repositioned the drill. "You've got five minutes. Starting now."

The front door creaked open.

"Leave them alone, Terrell. This is between us," Dalton said.

Dalton stood in the foyer, bag still on his head, but drooping to one side.

Mary's breathing was harsh, reminding him of bullet wounded brothers and sisters. "Shit. Fuck. What the sweet hell?"

"Mary, just breathe, okay," Harold said, tracing how far the blood ran down her neck, her wrists.

Dalton coughed, and scarlet spread across the front of the bag. "Do you deserve to kill me? Yes. But I'm already dead. Last I checked, everyone wants out. Show of hands, anyone?"

Terrell pointed the drill at him. "You fucked my life up. Not meth. I was clean. I had a wife. You—you—you fucking *gave* me to that thing. You have no idea what he did to me!"

Dalton placed his hands in his pockets. "I thought—"

"That's the problem, bro. Would I ever, ever touch your daughter? No. Not *any* fucking kid." Terrell said, shaking his head.

Dalton nodded. "It was Lumpton. I figured it out. I'm so sorry, Terrell."

"After you said: 'Oh, here's my best fucking friend.'"

"Stop!"Dalton exhaled. "I said I'm sorry."

Terrell's eye twitched, his jaw ticked. "Sorry?"

"I'm in the same boat. We all are." Dalton pointed outside the front door. "So is everyone in Shady Hills. If we work together, there's a chance."

Terrell exhaled. "Chance at what?"

"Getting out. Been trying for three years. Trial and error. *Who* we have here makes the difference. We strike tonight. We'll bring that thing down. He's gotten too wrapped up in his own ego and that thing he's building."

"It can't be that bright. Can't be *that* pretty," Terrell said.

Dalton shook his head. "Didn't say it would be. Best case? We all die. Except we *really* die. So do all those people in his garden."

"What if it doesn't work?" Terrell said.

"Would someone untie me?" Harold said.

Dalton walked up to Terrell, took the drill from him. "Terrell, untie them."

Mary squirmed in her chair. "Don't you dare come near me. I'll fucking rip your balls off!" She spat at him.

Carefully, Terrell untied her.

Mary grabbed the drill and knocked Terrell across the side of the head, dropping him.

"There," she said, and spat on him.

Harold pointed his head toward the hall. "He's got Dale tied up in there."

Dalton walked up to Mary. "We gotta work together."

She snapped at him, the sound echoed off the walls like a judge's gavel. "Fucker had a drill in my face."

"The Architect can die," Dalton said.

"What?" Harold and Mary said in unison.

Contemplating it, Dalton shrugged. "He's vulnerable sometimes. Like tonight. He's got something big planned."

Harold walked back into Dale's room, removed his gag and untied him. "You okay, Son?"

"Father of the year, Harold. Father of the year," Dale said, rubbing his wrists, his ankles.

Back on a first name basis. Great.

Harold took the bullet, feeling the pain of truth. *I can change this. It starts with—* He walked over to Dalton. "What aren't you telling us? No more secrets. What's up?"

Dalton exhaled. "We'll need mirrors, big and small, and everyone here. We start in the garden."

*****

Harold stubbed his cigarette out in the ashtray. "You okay, Terrell?"

Mary snorted. "Fuck him."

Terrell rubbed the side of his head. "Yo, I think I got a concussion."

"Oh, send a *wambulance*," Mary said.

Lighting a cigarette, Harold said, "Dalton, what's your plan?"

"We gotta move now. He's awakening what he's been building. He's got your father, Harold. He's key to whatever he's building. And boy he's pissed at me. I really fucked things up for him. So he'll want me for . . . something, I'm sure of that. We either stop it and bring it all down, or we get used to a *new* god."

Mary winced. "First part sounds great. Second part isn't ideal."

Harold motioned with his arm. "Why do we need mirrors?"

Dalton paced around for a few minutes. "In his garden there's a flower for each person that's dead or will be. When the moon is full, like tonight, they sprout from the ground, using the moon's help. We need a mirror for each of us. It will reflect the moonlight back.

Gives us the freedom we need. I know I'm grasping at straws, but that's how he feeds the flowers."

"And?" Harold said.

"The last thing The Architect said to me was that his masterpiece was asleep in the ground. Said it was like a giant, a god. It's in the ground, in and around the hollow. We cut in where the heartbeat is the faintest, and we find our way to the heart. Dale goes in first."

"Wait. Why Dale?" Harold said.

"He's the shortest, no offense," Dalton said. "Who else is about to go to medical school?"

Dale said, "Me. If I make it out of this."

Dalton gave him a light punch on his arm. "No one is safe, Dale. Even if you stay here or there, it's the same. Your father was right about one thing. Give him credit."

Dale ran back into his room. He returned holding his biology book. "I'll get you to where you need to be."

Harold lit a cigarette. "I mean, what do we do when we get there?"

Dalton meditated on it for some time, tapping the overturned table with his fingers. "After we get there? Close the connections, so to speak?"

"Yeah?" Mary said.

"The Architect was talking about waking that thing." Dalton shrugged his shoulders. "On this night, a long time ago, he found a way to cheat death."

Mary tied her hair back into a ponytail. "What does all of that mean?"

"It's tradition. With tradition comes rituals. I've seen him do them, know how important they are. We disrupt that, deliver a final blow."

"Final blow?" Harold said.

Dalton picked up his bag, pulled out a handful of C-4. "All we have to do is reach the heart, and, well, give it a heart attack. One it can't come back from. Again, grasping at straws here, but this is what I know from working for the son of a bitch. Got a drone, too. You still know how to operate those things, Mary?"

She laughed, rubbed at her wrists. "Ain't like the ones back in Iraq. More like a kid's toy, but it will help us scout it out."

Dalton slapped his hands on the table. "You got a better idea? Tonight is the night to do it. Any other night? Your odds are, I'd say, fucked. We all in?"

Harold looked at the faces around the table and the desperation weighed heavily on his heart. Especially Dale, who just sat with his arms folded, crying. *I won't fail you again, Son.*

Mary spoke up. "You know that thing better than we do."

Dalton jabbed his finger on the table for emphasis. "It's like when a spider molts. He's vulnerable. Arrogant, too. Should we do this, I just need to know one thing."

Harold scratched his goatee again. "What?"

"Why did you *really* save me back there?"

The migraine backed off. "You saved my life, and when we got back, you helped me get off the liquor. No one else believed in me."

"Then when the time comes, kill me. I want to rest in peace. Deal?" Dalton extended his hand. "Deal?"

Harold shook his hand. "Deal."

"Good. Now let's get ready. Time flies. But first," Dalton held his hand out. "Semper fi. Do or die."

Harold placed his hand atop Dalton's, and Mary

placed her hand above theirs. "Semper fi," they echoed. Terrell and Dale joined them.

Mary picked up the table and pushed her chair under it. "The Architect told me he was hungry. Does he mean for us, or what?"

Dalton laughed. "I hope we don't see."

CHAPTER 10

IT TOOK SOME time, but Harold managed to remove the mirror from his bathroom, as well as the one atop his dresser. Mary added two smaller ones from her purse while Dalton checked his bag to make sure he didn't leave anything behind.

Harold placed the last mirror carefully against the wall. He checked and packed two full magazines for his AR-15 in his pockets. *Rifle? Check. Ammo? Check. Ready to face death? Magic 8 Ball says ask again later.*

Mary shrieked.

Harold ran to her side, placed his arm around her. "What do you see?"

Tears began to flow down her cheeks. "My Mama. That son of a fucking bitch."

Her mother's face smiled at them in the mirror. "Come to Mama, sweetheart. I miss you so much, darlin'."

Dalton gave it a look. "We must go. *Now.*"

A quake started at the base of Harold's spine, working its way up to his head. In his mind's eye, he saw the village he and his fellow Marines walked into right before the ambush.

Stop it. Just stop.

Mary snapped her fingers. "Harold?"

"What?"

He realized she had been shaking him for some time. "Wake up. It's time to go."

Dalton zipped his bag up, rubbed his hands for warmth. "Sure is. Everyone got everything?"

Mary picked up one of the big mirrors, so did Dale. Harold slung his rifle over his shoulder. "Yep."

"Yo. If shit gets real—know what I'm sayin'—I just wanted to say I'm sorry."

"No need," Dalton said. "Still got that thing's drill?"

Terrell held it up and pulled the trigger.

"Good. Might come in handy. Okay, we do this by the numbers. Harold, you lead until we get to the hollow. Mary, you back up Harold. Dale, you take point once we're there. Terrell, keep your eyes and ears open and stay behind Mary," Dalton said. He took the bag off his head. He was pristine, like the day before he blew his brains out.

Mary wagged her finger in the air. "Hell's bells. How'd ya manage that?"

"For some reason, The Architect did it."

"Good to see your face again, brother," Harold said and hugged him.

Harold loaded a round in the chamber. "On me, let's go. You ready, Son?"

Dale held up his biology book. "Do we have a choice?"

"That's why we do it by the numbers and do it damn quick. Mary, get behind me. Dalton, you take up the rear with Dale and watch him. Terrell, don't lose us."

Opening the door, Harold prepared for the worst.

After watching a four-year-old girl, and four Marines die, he wondered what could be worse.

Oh, it's coming. Just bring them to me. To witness the atomic majesty.

Harold shook his head. *Fuck you and get out of my head.* He swung the door open, shouldered his AR, eyes scanning the streets for anything.

Nothing.

Harold made the hand motion to move. Slowly, they walked down the ramp and went behind the trailers, toward the hollow. Each step went about a foot into the ground, the snow crunching beneath them.

Steel twisting and tearing killed the silence. Harold made a fist and brought it up. They stopped. At the corner of Mr. Danvers' trailer, he peeked around the corner, then jerked back behind cover. "Shit," he whispered.

Dalton whispered back to him, "What is it?"

"Hard to tell, given it's so fucking dark. But it's bigger than the last one. We're gonna need some C-4," Harold said.

"For what?" Dalton moved ahead of Harold and peeked around the corner. "Oh."

"Get it ready," Harold whispered.

Mary, Dale, and Terrell joined them by the corner.

"What is it?" Mary whispered.

Harold placed his finger over his lips. "Something bigger than the last one."

A deep, guttural roar pierced the silence. They fell back against Harold's trailer and waited. Across the street, cement exploded, steel and chunks of drywall fell to the ground. Harold looked up and saw Mr. Danvers' trailer in the air, descending upon them. "Move!"

They ran to the nearest tree behind Harold's trailer. The crash reminded Harold of all the bridges he blew up back in Iraq. Pots, pans, and Mr. Danvers' satellite dish landed a few yards before them.

The dark shadow roared again, footsteps crushing the street beneath it. Another trailer flipped up into the air, crashing down like a controlled demolition.

"Get some C-4 ready," Harold said.

"Not that easy. You should know that," Dalton said.

Another roar filled Harold's head with white noise. He glanced back, taking in the ink-blot darkness which eclipsed the moon. It strafed them.

"Hey," Dale called out. He ran toward it, drawing the beast forward.

Harold stopped, turned around. "Dale?"

Pounding its way around what was left of Mary's trailer, it stopped before them. A large, pink tongue licked rows of teeth that glistened like broken piano keys in the moonlight. Its maw grew larger, ivory teeth circling like machinery. Saliva dripped, melting the ground around them.

Harold watched as Dale waved his arms at it. "Hello, fuck stick. Come get us!"

"Get back here," Harold whispered. "Fuck, he's gonna get killed. Dalton?"

Dalton reached into his bag and brought out four sticks of dynamite duct-taped together. He pulled out his zippo. He struck it and the wind put it out. He tried again, and again.

The shadow moved closer to Dale, licking its lips.

Dalton opened his jacket, giving the Zippo protection from the wind, and struck it again.

As soon as the wick sparked, Dalton threw it. "Shit. I didn't see Dale. Harold?"

Harold ran for Dale, collapsing on top of him, and wrapped his arms protectively around his boy. "Not tonight."

A deafening boom shook the ground. Entrails and hot liquid rained down, melting the snow. A whistle came from above, and Harold picked Dale up and ran back to them. The toilet shattered like fine china where Dale had stood.

"I can't lose you, Son. Not on my watch."

"You—you didn't have to do that," Dale said. "You saved me. You saved *us*."

The thing wailed like a wounded whale, holding its head in its hands, then fell over. Its tail went back and forth, smashing pieces of one of the trailers it threw, throwing up clouds of snow and dirt where it struck.

Harold reached out for Dale's hand. Crying, Dale took it. "Thanks, Dad."

Warmth spread in Harold's chest, allowing him to forget the winter for a few moments. He etched the moment in his memory. "Stick with me, Son."

"Yo. Think I just heard another one."

Dalton zipped his bag back up and got Harold to his feet. "Good enough. Run."

They made it to the last trailer before the forest and hunkered down. Every joint and ligament in Harold's body ached, his lungs raw from the November breeze. Snow fell and whipped around in every direction, blinding them.

Harold pulled his coat closed. "Is there anything here that doesn't want to kill us?"

Dalton snorted. "It's *him*. The Architect."

The wind howled as it grew in ferocity.

"Everyone okay?" Harold said over the din. He looked back, everyone was accounted for. "Nod if you're okay."

They nodded.

Harold took a knee, holding his rifle. "Dale, don't do that again."

Tears streamed down his face. "I'm sorry. And not just for this. For—"

"No time," Harold said. "Let's move."

What's taking everyone so long? Come on now, lads. Hurry it up, hurry it up.

Harold shook his head, freeing his thoughts. "Damn thing is in my fucking head again."

Dalton slapped him. "Name, rank, serial number. Keep running that through your mind. It gets worse, say them out loud, okay?"

He nodded.

Dalton pointed to the forest. "As long as there aren't any more of those, we all make it to the hollow."

Dalton unzipped his bag, pulled out a military trench shovel. "We'll need this."

Dale shrugged. "We dig into the capillaries. Follow that to the heart of the maze."

Harold coughed. "First the garden, or that thing will know we're coming."

Dale laughed. "It already does."

Yeah, I know.

CHAPTER 11

THE STORM INTENSIFIED as they trudged deeper into the forest. Harold's boots sunk deeper into the snow, slowing them down. This was The Architect's storm, which cut through his jacket, clothes, and skin. Burrowed into his marrow, until everything went numb. It stuck to the mighty oaks and birches, weighing them down. The branches creaked from the weight, about to split and fall. Boughs of the mighty oaks dropped clumps of snow, making him jump at the sounds as if an insurgent got the drop on them.

Pull it together. Now's not the time.

Off in the distance, gold and amber glowed. Over the treetops, focused moonlight spilled into the garden, feeding whatever grew there. A hidden garden, encircled by the largest of oaks, birches, and pines. The air reminded Harold of ozone.

"Stop," Harold said, bending over to catch his breath. Breath that looked like fog. He grimaced, shielding his eyes from the snow's tiny razors. "We're close. Damn, that's bright."

"Yo. How much more we got to go?" Terrell said.

Mary pointed toward the garden. "Not far."

Dale got his bearings. "Wait."

"What?" he said.

Dale pulled his hoodie tighter, then pointed toward the garden. "Do you feel that?"

"Feel what?" Harold said.

"Dig your feet into the snow, until they touch the ground. It's like a heartbeat."

Harold dug his boots in and felt it. "It's faint, but I feel it."

"Let's follow it," Dale said.

They followed the heartbeat, digging holes and gauging its strength, which brought them to the edge of the ancient trees encircling the garden. Some were redwood trees, as tall as the eye could see. Their majesty awed Harold. They were at least ten feet wide and God only knew how tall. They had no business being here. Pointing them out to Dalton, he said, "How?"

"Bastard can do whatever he wants. We're freezing. Let's move."

Harold measured his thoughts. "It should work."

"Wait," Dalton said, scratching his head. "*Should*?"

Harold sneezed. "You got a better idea?"

Dalton held his arm out. "Follow me. Don't look or talk to *them*."

"Them?" Mary said. "Whose *them*?"

"The flowers," Dalton said, pulling his trench shovel out of his bag. He handed it to Harold. "At least that's what that thing calls them."

Harold looked around for a place to sit. He found a snowbank and sat, instantly regretting it. The snow was freezing his testicles, so he stood up again. "It's too quiet."

Dalton patted Harold on the shoulder. "After you."

Harold unfolded the trench shovel, using it to separate the tall grass as he moved into the clearing. Entranced, he watched tendrils of moonlight caressing the ground up ahead. "Okay now what do we do, Dalton?"

Lightning peeled across the sky and kissed the ground close enough to send Harold wheeling to the ground. Struggling to get up, a sharp whine filled his head, drowning everything else out. He turned and only saw Dale, just as confused. He had his pinky fingers in his ears, opening and closing his mouth.

"Where are they?" Harold yelled.

Dale held his hands up, shook his head.

"Mary?" As soon as Harold said it, he regretted it. *What if that thing is listening?*

Dale motioned to where they entered, and Harold followed. The whine went away as quickly as it came, but the pain remained. Harold searched inside his coat's pockets for Excedrin. Finding it, he popped a few into his mouth and chewed them dry.

Never said this task would be easy, my good man.
Fuck you.

Harold waited for the sound of footfalls, but only heard his own erratic breathing; his heart beating a tattoo in his chest. He wondered what the tattoo would read. *You're fucked?*

"They've got to be back there," Harold said, walking out of the clearing back into the tall grass. When he reached the end, he could only see his and Dale's tracks in the snow. The wind picked up, moving the boughs above, dropping more snow.

"Dalton? Mary?" Harold called out into the night.
There are no tracks.

"Dad?"

Maybe they're inside?

"Yeah?"

"Where did they go?" Dale said.

"I don't know."

Harold walked up beside him and placed his hand on his son's shoulder. "Where to now?"

Dale pointed to where the tendrils of light shone upon a small garden. Even with the distance, some of the things which grew writhed in agony, their pale faces grimacing.

"Where do we start?" Harold said.

"The garden," Dale said, shivering.

"Here, we'll make it through."

"You trust Dalton and Terrell?"

"Thanks to that thing, it's hard to trust anyone *but* you." Harold cleared the snow from Dale's shoulders. "Stay behind me and be careful. You didn't see any weapons, or bags back there, did you?"

"No."

Harold turned and walked back into the tall grass. "We've got two mirrors. That's what matters."

As they approached the garden, Harold took in the sight before him: Tiny bodies resembling almost everyone that had died in Shady Hills grew from the ground, their faces shrouded by amber and gold petals. Inside each one, a twisted face screamed, scraping Harold's eardrums. Taking account of them, he noticed each had a rusted nameplate by them. Then he saw his father. The only flower not screaming.

Their eyes locked.

"Well, well. I knew you were stupid, but this? Where's your friends? You've given him everything he—"

Harold stomped the flower, but still, its twisted face stared up at him in horror.

He motioned to Dale. "Hand me the mirror."

Smoke escaped Oliver's mouth, spiraling up, and Harold remembered his brand of cigarettes. It was his brand, too. His guts churned.

"We've only got two, Dad. Where do we put it?"

Harold scanned the line of people—flowers, looking for himself or Dale. There were too damn many. He felt like he was spiraling down a drain.

Hold it. Keep it together.

"There," Harold said, pointing at his name plate, where a flower grew, but without a face. "Put a mirror there."

Dale did as he was instructed.

Harold stood there, waiting, but nothing happened.

"Dad? You okay?"

"I don't know, Son. Something should happen, right?"

Dale walked over to him. "I don't know either."

Harold watched his father sprout up again, choking on his smoke. "Smart move. But If you could put your pride away, we could work together—"

"Shut up, Oliver. Dale, move the mirror."

Dale handed him the mirror.

"Here," Harold said, taking the mirror from him. "It should go here." He placed the mirror in front of his father, which wilted to the ground as soon as he set it up. The wind picked up again, the tendrils from the moon lashed at the ground.

Time to move.

"Where is the entrance, Son? Just point it out."

Dale scanned the garden, mouth agape. He knelt down and began digging in the snow, clearing it away. "Feel that?"

Harold knelt down next to him and laid his hands on the ground. The heartbeat was strong enough to make him jump. He walked another ten yards in the same direction and dug his hands into the snow again. It was getting stronger, the rhythm more pronounced.

"See? It gets stronger the more we move this way."

Harold oriented himself.

Left arm, right arm, body.

Dale did the same in the opposite direction. Harold kept following the beat.

"There," Dale said, pointing at the oldest part of the garden. "That's gotta be its arm. We cut in, then we move to the heart."

"Let's dig," Harold said, unfolding the trench shovel. He pushed it into the snowy ground, placed his feet atop it, and began to dig. "How do we know when we hit it?"

Dale shuddered. "We'll know."

Harold made it past the snow and struck earth. He flung it off to the side, the air freezing his lungs. Each breath was harsher than the last. He sat down, caught his breath. Dale started digging with his hands where Harold left off.

"I found it," Dale said.

Harold got up, walked over to him, dug his hands in the ground. He pulled out his pocket flashlight and turned it on. Thick, gray flesh shimmered in the moonlight.

"Let's get this over with," Harold said.

They removed enough snow and dirt to reveal an arm about ten feet wide.

Veins pulsed inside, as the snow threatened to cover it back up. Harold hunched over and touched it, felt the heartbeat drum away.

"That's it," Dale said.

Harold shoveled the dirt around it out, marveling at how large it was.

That's gotta be ten feet wide, and at least five feet deep.

Dale pulled his biology book out of his backpack. "Looks like we're about to find out how good a doctor I'll become."

"Do your best, Son." Harold wiped sweat from his brow. "There's no opening. Do we just cut in?"

"Yes."

"Won't it know we're fucking around, I mean—"

"Yes," Dale said.

"It's gonna bleed all over the place. Shit . . . "

Scrambling, Harold pulled his pocketknife out, jumped into the hole, and began to cut. The only thing that bled out were fireflies and the stench of rotting corpses. Behind them, the flower's screams grew louder.

"Cut it wide enough for us," Dale said.

"Here we go."

CHAPTER 12

Holding the slit open, Harold motioned for Dale. "I'll be right behind you."

Dale dipped into the hole and slid inside. Harold followed. The insides felt like raw steak and stank of death. Blue and red veins pulsed against translucent skin. Fireflies flew past them, lighting the way, and clotting the cut he made. With every thump, more fireflies came. Keeping time with the infernal rhythm. They flowed like blood.

Harold closed his eyes, his hands prying them off his face. "Dale?"

"Dad?"

It brought back memories of boot camp. Crawling under barb wire blind was part of his training, and just like the barb wire, sometimes you got bit and caked with mud. This wasn't mud though. Remnants of the dead lined the tunnel. *Don't think about it. Just move.*

"Ouch," Harold said, slapping his arm. A warm, iridescent goo spread across his hand and arm.

Dale motioned for him to follow. "This way."

Just like that drill, Harold found himself crawling on his belly, ducking his head. Slick goo he was glad he couldn't see coated his arms, his belly. He opened his eyes and saw Dale struggling. "Crawl on your belly and keep your head down."

Dale's hands found purchase, pulling him farther along.

A little way up, the fireflies disappeared, revealing a familiar face. Sheriff Lumpton's body was suspended in the air, drawn taut by his nerves, reaching as far as Harold could see, forming the tendon of the arm they had crawled inside. His vivisected body hummed like a guitar string when the tendon moved. "Help me."

"We don't help child molesters. You get what you deserve," Harold said.

Flesh from Lumpton's face stretched so far Harold could almost see through it. Without the uniform, Harold would've never known. He couldn't make out the poor soul connecting with him ahead. Lumpton's nerves interlocked with the nerves of other bodies, connected to muscles attached to the railway lined skeleton. Atop them sat those perfect spheres. Lightning flashed inside them, jerking nerve and tendon alike. A nervous system of the dead; one part of the god The Architect had spent over a hundred years building.

Dale's breathing scared him. If he wasn't careful, he would pass out. *Or pop. It's possible.*

Harold crawled through the mess of bodies toward Dale and touched his shoulder. "Just keep moving. There's nothing we can do for them."

"We'll end up like this," Dale said, snorting back tears. "We can't end up like this. We—we—have to—"

"Dale." Harold shook him. "Get a hold of yourself. We're almost there."

Dale nodded, then moved again. Harold followed.

The tunnel became larger as they moved. More fireflies sped past them in a crimson and gold symphony, some of them smacking Harold in the face. Gripping the spongy, warm flesh of the vein, Harold pulled himself along, keeping pace with Dale. Whoever was connected to Lumpton terminated in a massive ball made of bodies in different stages of decay. He retched on the scent of death and sewage. Dale threw up.

The tendon creaked as the ball moved as one cohesive unit. Children made up the center, the elderly folded around them in positions the human body wasn't built to endure. A child's face was in the center, like a hubcap. It opened its eyes, double pupils spinning. Its smile turned into a grimace, its bone-white tongue licking split lips. Everything Harold had seen back in Iraq paled in comparison. He was shaking again, making it hard for him to grab the vein and pull himself forward.

"Can I play with your son?" The child's face said. "We'd have a fun old time."

Dale shrieked.

"Dale?"

Dale turned and looked at him, all the color left his face.

"You're going into shock. Breathe. Okay?"

Nothing.

Harold slapped him, bringing him back. Dale gasped for air, lungs pumping.

"Don't look. Just move forward. Right?"

"Don't look," Dale said, "just move forward."

"Yeah. Just don't look, buddy."

"Okay," Dale said, pulling his shirt over his mouth and nose.

Harold watched the child's face, its eyes following them as they moved along. "You're no fun. I want to play. I want to play!"

Dale stopped, and Harold nudged him. "Don't listen to it."

"That's Tommy. We used to go to school together. He let me play with his lightsaber. Isn't there something we could do? Put him out of his misery?"

"I don't know, but we'll find out. Just keep moving."

They moved around the bend of the shoulder, Dale carefully gauging which vein to use. "This one goes straight to the heart," Dale said, pointing the way.

"Go."

The creaking of the countless bodies grew louder as if the creature holding them were moving. It felt like an elevator ride. Up and down. Up and down. Harold had to keep pushing Dale forward so they wouldn't slide back down the way they came.

The vein branched off to an artery as big as a plantation-style mansion, which shrank and grew in rhythm with its heartbeat. The tunnel vibrated in sync with it, making Harold's teeth chatter. It reminded him of hearing his son's heartbeat in utero, except this was amplified, building pressure inside his skull.

"Dale?"

"What?"

Harold joined him. "What have we got?"

Dale took stock. "A shovel and a knife."

Tightening his grip on the shovel, Harold said, "Then we'll cut the fucking thing's heart out. We don't quit. We. Do. Not. Give. Up."

"I know, but—."

"Think of Mary, Son."

"What if we disappear? Like Mary, Dalton, and Terrell?"

Harold caressed Dale's cheek, smiled. "Then we go down fighting." Harold hugged him. "I've run away from a lot of things in my life, but not you."

"I—I can't lose you again, Dad," Dale said, wiping snot from his nose.

Soothing warmth filled Harold, emanating from his heart, as it knitted itself back together.

I broke the vicious cycle.

"You won't lose me, Son."

A low moan echoed past them.

Dale's eyes grew and his pupils dilated.

"We do this together. Stay behind me and hold my hand," Harold said.

"Okay."

"Never let go."

Dale wiped tears from his cheeks. "I won't."

Harold took his hand and squeezed as hard as he could without hurting him.

They followed the moans to where the artery opened into the aorta. Harold brought them to a stop. "We move *slow*, okay?"

Dale nodded.

Peeking around the corner, Mary sat in an old wooden chair, blocking their path. Hands tied to the arms, her head down, hair the color of wheat spilled across her lap. Her back rose and fell in hitches with each breath.

Harold moved slow, ready for anything. Placing his back to the artery's wall, Dale's hand in his, they moved closer to the pipe which opened into the heart itself.

As they approached her, Harold squeezed Dale's hand. "Mary?"

Shaking her face free of hair, Mary looked up at them. "Harold?" she whispered.

They ran to Mary only to find her shackled to the chair with ropes of fine leather. Harold tried untying the leather across her wrists, her ankles, only to watch it cinch back down, harder and harder, cutting deep into her flesh. "Stop," she said in agony, defeated.

Digging in his pocket for his knife, Harold said, "We're not leaving you here."

"It's too late. He's waiting for you. Both of you."

He looked at Dale as if that would answer it. "Both of us? Why would—"

"He told me," Mary said.

Harold ran her hair behind her ears, cupped her face. "What did he say?"

Mary's eyes found his. "That his masterpiece is almost done."

"How?"

"I know you love me, and I love you." She sobbed. "Ain't none of that'll matter if that son of a whore wins. Do it for me, Harold. Do it for us. Do it for everyone in Shady Hills."

Her words were like a hammer striking his head, ringing his bell. "I love you more than you know, but we're all making it out of this. Trust that," Harold said, stroking her face.

Mary bit her lip, turned her face. "Semper Fi, Marine." She nodded. "This is our only chance. Make it count, soldier." She shuddered.

Harold kissed her. "Semper Fi, Marine."

Dale hugged her. "We can all make it out. Right, Dad?"

Mary shook her head. "Dale, do what your dad says. Ain't no use but giving it your all. This . . . *thing* of his comes alive, we're done."

"I know. I won't let you down," Harold said.

Mary looked at him as if she was trying to solve the world's most complicated math problem. "Please don't leave me like this."

Harold whispered in her ear, "We're going to kill it. There's a reason he wants us. A reason we're alive. And we'll *stay* alive."

Mary looked at him with all the hope of a dead woman. "Don't let him trick you."

"He needs all of us. Dale and I saw them on our way in." Cold, shaking fingers ran through his goatee. "Where's Dalton? Terrell?"

"I don't know about Terrell, but he got Dalton. With you and Dale? He'll be able to wake up this *thing*. Don't fuck this up."

"We'll put an end to that," Harold said.

Mary strained against her bindings. "You saw what it's capable of, Harold. Please."

He took a deep breath. "I don't trust The Architect. There has to be a way."

He thought long and hard, tears running down his cheeks, as he stared at her. Reaching, grasping for a plan, a solution.

Nothing. Except pure faith and perseverance.

What did that get you back in the desert?

He reeled against the thought. It wasn't his. It was a British accent in his head.

Come on in, lad. See my masterpiece.

Harold shook his head.

"Dad?" Dale said. "Are you okay?"

As the heartbeat grew louder, smoke flowed with it. It was from a familiar brand of cigarettes.

"Shit. It's Oliver. He's the heart," Harold said. "Forgot about that."

Right, then. I cordially invite the both of you to bear witness to the awakening of a god.

Harold took Dale's hand. "You ready, Son?"

Dale nodded.

Hand in hand, they walked toward darkness, and fell.

Everything went dark as they descended like an elevator with its wires cut.

CHAPTER 13

HAROLD AND DALE landed on their asses, cushioned by myriad veins, sewn together with tendons. They stood up. Orange and gold flickered as the fireflies flew about, illuminating a door made of flesh. Dead eyes stitched into the door stared at them, milky and white. The door glistened, like a fresh wound with blood seeping from its cracks and crevices. Its handle, made of weathered teeth, with barb wire for gums, grinned at them. Harold approached it, wrapping his hand in a handkerchief. It sprung open, teeth surrounding a hungry black hole. A bloody tongue lolled out, licking the blood and sucking it in. Pink ran down the corners of its mouth, dripping on the floor.

Harold pulled his hand back.

Dale tugged on his jacket. "Dad?"

"Stand back. I'm kicking it in."

Gaining the proper distance, Harold told himself it was just like the doors he kicked down in Iraq, as heavily fortified as they were. He gave it his all.

Nothing.

Pain shot up his leg, his knee buckled. "Fuck," he whispered, even though he had the nagging suspicion they were being watched.

The door opened enough for The Architect to stick his head out. He looked at the door, then Harold. "You could have just knocked, my good man."

Harold raised the barrel of his AR-15, sighted it between The Architect's eyes, and fired.

The shot went straight through, the entrance wound sealing itself, helped by the fireflies.

"What's all this then?" The Architect opened the door fully, motioned for them to enter. "I'm glad you have proven yourself, Mr. Stoe. Your son as well." He took a deep breath, holding his arms out. "Look at what I've finished. You are looking at my life's work. Took a lot of people, and a lot of time. But it's," The Architect looked around the inside of his creation's head, "perfect. Absolutely. Perfect."

Harold let go of Dale and sighted the rifle on the huge brain above. More bodies in differing states of decay were balled up with electrical wiring which sparked erratically. Like a Rubik's cube, it churned, making a chugging sound as the pistons and crankshafts moved the bodies and parts around above them. Engine exhaust filled the room, smelling like a mechanic's shop with a butcher's nearby. The floor was tiled in bone, honed to a sheen. To the right of them, two round and large pieces of glass shimmered. Bodies filled them, too.

The Architect wagged his finger, made a *tsk-tsk* sound. "Can you not see your guns are useless?" The smile split his face, fireflies crawling out, fretting about his waxen features.

"This—this is—" Harold managed, lost in awe at the spectacle before him.

Pointing toward the large, transparent circles,

which comprised the eyes, The Architect said to them. "Forever asleep, but after pulling the moon closer, it will finally awake." The Architect shook his head. "It has taken me over one-hundred-and-fifty years to complete." Tears of pride ran down his cheeks and patted on the floor.

Harold still looked about, taking in the splendor. "Why?"

Placing his hands behind him, The Architect walked up to Harold. "We both know how your world will end without my intervention. We crest a new cycle, a cycle full of extinction—engineered of greed. Society is breaking down, and your eyes are too young to remember. Everything *will* break down without my intervention, of course. You see it all around you—the beginning of it. Everyone is tearing everyone apart. Now, it doesn't have to be that way." The Architect turned Harold toward the behemoth's cold, large eyes. "Look around. Your proper-fucked, and you know it. It's our turn now, Mr. Stoe, and what we'll create—"

"Fuck you."

"No room for pessimism, my lad. Only reverence, for a god that I have given flesh."

Squinting, Harold saw Dalton's body filling in the center of the left eyeball, twisted in a tight fetal position.

"You both served and saw the worst in this world. Now you will serve me and my creation. Bear witness as we lay the heavy hands of change upon this cesspool. We will reshape *everything*."

"My son and I aren't going any—"

"Your son will keep my daughters company." The Architect chuckled. "This is beyond you. You have only one role to fill. Now then, if you'll excuse me, I am to be its mind. First." The Architect reached up, grabbing a stray wire from the mess above him. A spark danced between his fingers. He touched it to the nerve of the great combination above him. Bodies shook. Engines roared to life.

Harold watched as the spark became lighting, caressing the bodies, cogs, and engines. In front of him, the eyes slowly opened into darkness.

The Architect pulled a pocket-watch from his vest. "Ah," he said and placed it back. "Time to wake it up. I took the liberty of writing a song for this occasion. I'm sure I'm a bit rusty, as I made the violin so many years ago."

A spine from a child appeared in his left hand, a bow in his right. Tiny ribs jutted from the sides, curved upward to secure nerves that quivered in anticipation of his touch. The Architect brought the bow across the nerves and began to play. A chorus of screams filled the room as if its owners were burning alive. Harold tried to make sense of the voices, but the agony, the death rattles, were so loud, their pressure almost burst his eardrums.

As The Architect played the song, sobs, wails, and cries replaced the lamentations of the charred. His fingers moved so fast they were a blur, bringing nuance. Cries of babies ripped from their cold, dead, mothers' arms, added to the cacophony.

Bringing the ill song to a crescendo, an atomic explosion filled Harold's head, ending the pain, the suffering of the dead. After, winds scattered his thoughts, blowing them around as winter scatters leaves. Every bone in Harold's body hummed along.

Once the song was over, The Architect's tongue teased the nerves, licked the bow, cleaning it as a mother cat would a kitten. Especially where the nerves were the fattest. The violin vanished with the bow.

The Architect gave them a humble bow.

"Now that's a proper way of waking a god. I call it, *The End*. Cheers!"

Gripping Dale, Harold felt the earth move beneath the abomination. Perfect spheres encasing atomic explosions on pause floated about like soap bubbles. Some went upward, into the brain, while others danced around The Architect.

Bodies of the dead moved in unison as The Architect's creation slowly unearthed itself. Freeing itself from the earth below, the roar shook the room. The sound of skyscrapers falling almost burst Harold's eardrums. The Architect's masterpiece up-rooted trees and stone alike. He and Dale backed up against the wall so they wouldn't fall. That elevator feeling again. When the creation's eyes opened, Harold saw the garden to one side, the hollow to another, as they rose, tearing the earth to shreds until it stood tall over the redwoods.

Like a conductor, The Architect reached upward, pulling, squeezing certain synapses, puppeteering it. "Nothing like a fresh start, eh, Harold?"

Finally, the noise stopped. The creation swayed in the November breeze on unsteady legs.

Harold tried to squeeze the trigger, but he was frozen. Styrofoam filled his throat. He tried to speak, but it expanded. His heartbeat filled his ears.

"*Girls?* I found a new friend for you," The Architect said.

"Father?" They said in unison.

Crawling on their hands and feet, Harold saw the cogs and pistons jutting from their backs and through old, tattered dresses, squealing in protest as they entered the room. They had all the grace of wind-up toys, hands and feet striking the bone floor in a clockwork rhythm. Coming to a halt, their heads twisted upward, staring at Harold and Dale. What hair was left on their liver-spotted scalps hung in front of doll-like faces, cracked and splintered with age. Each eyeball was a different color, bugging out of their faces.

"Caroline, Samantha, this is Dale. Dale, this is Caroline and Samantha."

The Architect motioned toward them. "Don't be shy or afraid," he said, helping them to their feet. Their dresses fit their emaciated bodies, cheeks sunken, eyes set in dark calderas. They shuddered as they walked, the cogs and pistons doing their job.

"He's more afraid of you, remember? We talked about this." The Architect ran his fingers through Caroline's hair, shaking the strands that came out to the floor until there was little left.

Samantha coughed, spilling black oil to the floor. "What—what game," she took a deep breath, smoke escaping through her mouth, her nose, "do you want to play first?"

Harold saw Dale out of the corner of his eye. He was frozen in place.

"Let's make a maze," Dale said.

They cocked their heads to the side. "A maze?"

Dale blinked at his father. "I'll show you how."

The Architect approached Harold. "I'm disappointed in you, Mr. Stoe. I fixed you, your son, and your love, and this is how you repay me? Be a good lad, it's time for you to serve. Like that back-stabbing Dalton." He wrapped his arms around Harold. "Take your place. Easy now, let me help. That's a good lad."

Harold started to walk, The Architect helping him along.

No. Mission failure. Abort. Abort.

The Architect placed his arm around Harold and walked him up to the right eye. "You will only need your eyes. What you will see," The Architect's mouth spread open, barb wire teeth teased the air, "will be everything I ever dreamed of. You will remember everything. Look upon what *I* will build."

"Dad?" Dale said.

"I love his hair," Caroline said to Samantha as she toyed with it. "Father? Can we have his hair?"

The Architect stopped and turned to them, meditated. "Why not? Share and share alike."

Samantha pulled out a pair of rusted scissors. "What about his face?"

"Dad?" Dale cried out.

"Why not?" The Architect said.

Harold grabbed the thing's throat and squeezed until the color drained out of its face. The Architect just smiled.

Once they got close to the eye, The Architect folded Harold into a fetal position, and placed him inside the eye. "We've got you sorted out now, Mr. Stoe. Now just watch. *Forever.*"

Nerves and tendons wrapped around Harold's body, threatening to suffocate him. Keeping him in place. He tried to move, but it was worthless.

"Dad?"

Managing to turn his head, he watched The Architect's daughters chase Dale around.

"Wait," Dale said, pulling a pencil from his pocket. "If you can get yourself out of the maze, you win. I lose? You get to have my hair *and* my face. Okay?"

They considered it. "Okay."

As The Architect crept up the stairs and into the tangled mess comprising the brain, he gave Harold one last glance. "Time to raise the tides and split the earth."

Struggling to unfold himself within the crystalline eyeball, Harold watched as a great, luminous hand rose and grabbed the moonlight itself, twisting it into tendrils attached to the moon, pulling it closer. What was left of the earth shook beneath them. Wails of countless dead, straining from the effort, echoed up to his ears.

Just what in sweet hell do I do now?

Barely audible, Dalton whispered from the other eye, "You get your ass out of there. I've only got one block of C-4 left. Better make it count."

Bending his arm in a way he shouldn't, Harold popped it out of its socket. He screamed his throat raw. Groaning, he pulled his pocketknife from his pants pocket and began to cut the muscles and chords which held him in place.

"Quick," Dalton whispered.

Harold sliced through one of the muscles holding him in place, giving him a little more leverage. As he continued to cut, he looked over his shoulder at Dale, drawing a maze on a sheet of paper. The Architect's daughters stood in rapt attention.

Another great hand covered the creation's eyes, and the god howled as it came alive. What trees, dirt, and snow were left, were uprooted and flew like confetti in the wind. Cutting the last chord, Harold fell to the floor. He tried to stand but his strained back wouldn't allow it.

"Crawl over here," Dalton said.

Harold crawled on his belly to Dalton. "Give it to me."

Dalton wriggled and strained. "Fuck. Can't reach it."

"You have to."

Harold reached for Dalton, and once he got a handful of his coat, he pulled himself up. Cutting Dalton's bindings with his pocketknife, he freed Dalton enough for him to hand Harold the C-4.

"Don't fuck it up, Harold. When you get to the heart, just press the button. You've got thirty seconds."

With a flourish, The Architect appeared. "I leave you two alone for a few minutes and look at what I find. Do you know how long it will take to fix the damage? Here," The Architect took the C-4 from Harold, "let me help."

The Architect pressed the button. Nothing happened.

Examining the device, The Architect said, "The wires have been snipped." He dropped the C-4 to the floor. "In time, Mr. Stoe, you will learn to love what I have built. Until then—"

The Architect stomped on Harold's ribs.

Harold screamed, feeling—and hearing—his ribs break. It was like someone shoved a hot iron rod into his side. Spots danced before his eyes.

"How dare you meddle." The Architect drew a sharp breath. "You cannot undo what's been done." He kicked his broken ribs again.

Even the scream hurt. All Harold could do was lay there and concentrate on breathing, which came out as an asthmatic whine. Everything else was eclipsed by pain. He swam in and out of consciousness. He tasted pennies.

The Architect straightened his coat, his tie. "There. That should do it." Then he kicked the C-4 off to the side. Eyes shut, face grimacing, Harold didn't see where it went. All he could hear was The Architect's footsteps as he ascended the stairs.

I fucked up, again. Dale, I'm so very sorry. I—I—

"Shhh."

Harold opened his eyes and saw Dalton sitting next to him, C-4 in hand. "I cut the wires on purpose. Only way to get it inside without *him* knowing. Let me see your knife."

Harold coughed and saw bright, crimson dots hit Dalton's face. "You couldn't even wire a toaster. We both know that. Get me up. Slowly."

Dalton reached under Harold's armpits and pulled him up.

Harold screamed, making it worse.

Shaking, Harold took the C-4 in his hands, and with his knife, began to strip the wires.

"Careful. Don't cut the wires, just strip them. I don't have any spares," Dalton said.

"No shit," Harold said.

"This maze looks familiar," Caroline said, running her finger over the sheet of paper.

Dale brushed his hair out of his eyes. "Then it shouldn't be hard to finish."

Again, Dale blinked at his dad.

"Hurry," Dalton whispered.

"There," Harold managed, showing Dalton the stripped wires. "Now—" Harold coughed again, feeling the razors cutting into his lungs, his stomach. "Just gotta twist them back together. Hit the button."

Blind, The Architect's creation's hand felt for and found the tendrils of the moon and pulled again. The room became brighter. The moon became bigger.

Dalton snatched the C-4 from Harold and twisted the wires together. "Not here. It won't work." He pointed to Dale. "Wait for it."

Biting his lower lip, Dale watched Caroline and Samantha work their way through the maze. "You're almost out."

"I get to cut his hair and his face." Caroline said.

Samantha put her hand over the paper. "Hey. This looks a lot like Dad's—"

"It's Dad's—it's—it's the way to—" Caroline said.

The Architect appeared from nowhere, cleared his throat. "To the god's heart. Nice try, little man, but not enough."

Caroline pointed to a section of the paper. "There. Now it's solved."

Dale ran over to Harold, placed his arm around him, protecting him.

With the wires twisted, and the red LED light shining on the block of C-4, Dalton grabbed Harold by the coat, and pulled him along toward the door as fast as he could. Dale followed.

Harold let out another scream, blood following it. It dripped down the sides of his mouth.

Dalton let go of them and slammed into the door. Nothing.

The Architect made that *tsk-tsk* sound again. "I

underestimated you, Dalton." He walked toward them. "I thought this was what you wanted. Your freedom? A final resting place?"

Dalton kept launching himself at the door, trying to bust it open.

"Fuck you," Dalton said.

The Architect's eyes began to spin again. "*Fuck me?*"

Dalton burst through the door.

Stifling laughter, The Architect called after them, "The heart is your father, Harold. Best of luck working with him."

CHAPTER 14

"STOP," HAROLD MANAGED through rapid, short breaths. He slapped Dalton's hand away from his shoulder and leaned up against the wall. "I can't make it. But Mary and Dale can."

"That's what *I* said back in Iraq, in that village. You don't leave a Marine behind." Dalton grabbed Harold by his coat and gently pulled him toward the chair Mary sat in. "Dale, where to and how far?"

Dale scoured his biology textbook. "We're close. Uhmmm." Looking about, Dale got his bearings. "This way."

Gold and amber illuminated Mary. Like snakes, the bindings slithered around her wrists and ankles. "You don't look good, Harold," she said.

Harold coughed through the laughter. "Makes two of us. Dalton?" He wiped blood from his mouth.

"I'm on it," Dalton said, pulling Harold against the wall of the artery.

Dalton motioned for Dale to help him with Mary. He handed the kid a knife he had stashed in his boot and placed his blade just under her wrists. Dale did the same.

"On the count of three," Dalton said. "One. Two. Three."

They cut, and Mary raised her arms as the dead leather strained for her.

"Her ankles," Dalton said.

Same maneuver.

"One. Two. Three," Dalton said.

They cut and Mary fell forward. Dalton caught her in his arms, dragged her over to Harold.

Dalton bent over, catching his breath, his strength. "Mary? Can you walk?"

With effort, she made it to her feet, body swaying. "I think so."

"Help me with Harold. Dale?" Dalton said.

"I know. It's this way. Come on," Dale said, pointing the way.

The door opened. A shadow of The Architect fell across the floor of the artery. "It won't work, lads."

Dalton grabbed Harold under one arm, Mary the other. "Run."

"Run, indeed." The cackle reminded Harold of metal wasps. "I've need for musical instruments where we're going."

Harold wheezed.

Hold it together, Marine. Hold it together.

"Yo! Look what I got," Terrell said.

Harold turned and saw him standing behind The Architect, shimmering drill in hand.

The Architect snarled. "That is mine, nig-nog." He held his hand out. "Give it to me. Now."

"This?" Terrell pressed the trigger of the drill and pushed it into The Architect's chest. "Say nig-nog again, mother fucker." The drill whined in protest as blood and little pieces of machinery hit the walls. The Architect grabbed Terrell's hand, trying to wrench the drill free.

"Harold," Dalton said. "Now's our chance. He's weak. Come on."

"Hey," Mary called. "Ass clown. Over here."

Harold managed to slide up the wall. He took one step after another, each filled with the sensation of his lungs being sliced, his back about to break again. "This ends now."

Dalton grabbed the trench shovel from his bag, unfolded it, and hit The Architect in the back of the head. A metallic clang echoed. He watched as skull fragments and cogs fell from the widening crack.

The Architect stumbled backward, eyes spinning in opposite directions. "You—You, can't . . . win," he stammered. In one swift motion, The Architect grabbed the drill from Terrell. He held it back as if to brain him with it.

Mary grabbed The Architect's hand. "No, sweetie. Not today." She wrenched it free and drilled through The Architect's forehead. The sound of an old dentist's drill filled the hallway. The Architect's body shook as if a thousand volts were put through it.

Finally, his eyes stopped spinning. He staggered towards them, one hand holding the back of his head, the other holding the front. "My life—my life is in this . . . god." He smiled, blood flowing from the corners of his split lips.

Mary took a few steps back, grabbed the neck of Harold's coat and pulled him away. Terrell ran up to help.

Harold coughed up more blood. Pinpricks danced along his arms and legs. "Son, take us to the heart."

The Architect fell to one knee. His head jerked to the left, then to the right, as more cogs, oil and blood spilled from his forehead. "Good luck with your father, Harold." He slapped his knee and laughed like a hyena. "There's no stopping this."

"This way," Dale said and ran. Mary pulled Harold along with the help of Dalton and Terrell.

Through twists and turns, they found the main valve of the heart, where all paths ended in a giant, pink membrane with a Y cut into it. It opened, puffs of smoke hung in the air. Then it closed and stayed that way.

Dalton wiped the blood from Harold's mouth. "You're the only one who can do this. Make it right."

Dale knelt next to Harold. "Forgive him. Like I forgave you."

"You have no idea what that son of a bitch did," he said, shaking his head.

"Back in the garden, he said he wanted to work with us, but you just stomped him down. We *need* him, Dad."

Harold closed his eyes, searching for good memories of his father. Finally, he found the one at the playground. His father had pushed him in the swing. "Faster," Harold had cried. Right before the swing threw him, his father had caught him. Took him into his arms.

Harold placed his hand on the thin membrane. "Dad. We need to talk."

The three pieces of flesh burped. More smoke exited, creating a cloud.

"I'm not here for just me." Harold coughed up more blood. "I'm here for everyone, and I'm here to say you're right. You were right about everything."

The Architect's footsteps were close.

The valve of the heart opened again. "Go on," Harold's father said.

Harold sighed. "You did the best you could. You— you got clean and sober later, looked after Mom for all those years. I'll never forgive myself for not attending your funeral." Tears flowed freely. "Uncle tried to tell me how you took care of everything, and Mom's funeral. What kind of man you were, and what kind of man you became, but I just focused on the bad times. It's all my fault."

The valve opened.

Creak-creak-creak.

"Son? You okay?"

Harold waved him off. "I was stupid and pissed off at myself. Just as much as you were. Yeah, you were a bag of dicks, Dad. But when it mattered, you were there."

"Hell, that pig-fucker will be here soon. Is that C-4 I smell?" Harold's father said.

Dalton handed Mary the controls to the small quadcopter drone he'd bought at a 7-Eleven and attached the C-4 to the bottom of it. "Mary?"

She began to back away but stopped.

"Mary?" Harold said. "Look at me."

When she did, he saw a glimmer of strength.

The Architect's footsteps were closer.

"It's the past we're fighting. Let it die. It's the only way. You can do it," Harold said.

Mary looked at the controller and pressed the ON button. Dalton pressed the button on the C-4 and let go as it flew into the air, bumping against the membrane.

Harold tried to stand but fell on his butt. "I'm so sorry, Dad. Please. Open up."

"I'm sorry too, Son," Oliver said as the valve opened. "Can't hold him off for long."

Mary guided the drone through the valve and into the aorta. "Fuck yeah. Still got it!"

"Now what? We all die or—" Harold said.

"Lads and lasses. What. Have. You. Done?" The Architect said. One hand on the wall, the other covering his forehead. "You can't stop a god."

"No," Harold coughed and spat the blood that came with it on The Architect. "Just its heart."

The Architect moved past them toward the valve. "Oliver? Oliver, please." He pleaded, banging his fists on the valve, waiting for it to open again.

Dale stopped them. "We don't get out of here, we're dead. Dad? You okay?"

Harold pointed upward. "No."

Mary lifted him some. "Does that feel better, sugar?" He glanced into her face and saw the most beautiful thing the world had ever shown him.

"A little," he said.

"Dale, can we get out of here?" Dalton said. "We've only got thirty seconds."

Dale thought for a minute, rubbed his chin. "Follow me."

Mary shrieked.

They dropped Harold. Ice picks pierced his chest.

I'm dead. Either way, I'm dead.

"That's what you get, you cunt," The Architect said.

Harold turned and saw the tip of a blade sticking out from the side of Mary's chest. Crimson bloomed on her dress.

Oh, no.

"*You. Wee little bastard,*" The Architect said.

Dalton grabbed The Architect's arms. "Go on. I'll hold him back. Either way, I'm finally dead, finally at peace."

Dale grunted as he pulled Harold along the winding path to where the vein was closest to flesh, Mary and Terrell holding up the rear. "The shoulder. We can make it. This way."

"Give me the shovel," Dale said, grabbing it from Harold.

Dale unfolded it and sliced at the top.

The vein opened.

A deafening boom moved through them, emanating from the chest, and echoing through the body.

"Fuck," Mary said. "Harold?"

"Here," he said, lifting his hand again.

Shockwaves rumbled through the body, tearing the connections between the bodies comprising it. Flesh, nerves, and bone strained, splintered, ripped. Pistons and cogs tore through the wall of bodies. One tendon snapped, barely missing Harold's face. To Harold, it felt like the elevator was falling again. The ceiling was caving in.

Dale threw the shovel. "Now!" He jumped, holding onto the shoulder bone, and pulled himself up. Dale dropped a rope made of nerves and tendons.

Mary pulled Harold underneath it, then jumped. She caught it, tried to pull herself up.

He took in as much breath as he could. "Pull, Mary, pull."

She struggled slowly up the rope, panting, wheezing.

Once she was clear, Harold saw them dangling the rope. "Come on, Dad."

"Go on," Harold said to Terrell.

"You first, man," Terrell said.

Just let it go. You've done your duty. She won't love you. You'll never have a normal life.

"No, Dad, no."

Harold grabbed the rope. Mary and Dale pulled him up while Terrell pushed Harold's ass upward. Harold's chest filled with November air, each breath like a knife slashing what was left of his lungs.

"Terrell?" Harold called down the open slit.

Terrell jumped and grabbed the rope, pulled himself up and out of the monstrosity.

Dale pointed at the garden and said, "Look."

Standing on the shoulder of a giant god, they watched as its massive hand let go of the moon's tendrils and drop to its side. The moon became smaller, more distant, replaced by the rising sun. Perfect spheres floated out of its mouth, dispersed by the sun's rays. Below, stretching as long and far as Shady Hills itself, a great pit the size of a god lay before them.

"Good show. Good show. I just," The Architect said, pulling himself up through the slit to join them, "wanted to see one last sunrise before I—"

Harold watched The Architect's eyes dim, its head lolling on his shoulder. The first rays of the sun melted his flesh, exposing a metal skeleton, surrounded by organs stitched together in precise manners.

The would-be god began to tilt forward.

We did it. We actually did it.

"Hold on tight, guys," Harold said. He sunk his hands into the shoulder's flesh. "I think we're in for a doozy."

Dale, Mary, and Terrell did the same.

The aberration fell to its knees, bucking Harold and his crew. Harold cried out and so did Mary. The sun's rays hit the treetops below them.

"When this thing falls, grab the nearest tree and hug it," Harold said. "Just like parachute training . . . if it went wrong."

The Architect's masterpiece, which took over a hundred years to make, began to fall apart, dumping bodies everywhere, filling in the pit it rose from.

The treetops were close enough for Harold to see a startled squirrel staring at him. "Now!"

As Harold struck a tree, the world went black.

***

"Breathe. You're not gonna die. Breathe!" Harold could barely hear the flight medic over the rotors of the helicopter.

"Cough!"

Harold did. Blood came up.

"I'm gonna roll you on your side. Your lung's collapsed. It's gonna hurt!"

It was like being stuck with an icepick. Cold, harsh air entered his lungs as he breathed.

Flap-flap-flap, they went.

"You're gonna be okay. We're almost to the hospital"

Harold passed out again.

***

"Dad?"

Blinding light hurt his eyes. Holding his arm over his face as a shield, everything slowly came back to him. The sun—the warm sun. Mary and Dale holding his hand. Then, movement. Lights strobing his eyes.

The taste of the anesthetic gas was still in his mouth. Finally, the hospital room swam into focus.

"Dale?" Harold managed.

"Dad," Dale said, wiping the hair out of his face. "You want a drink of water?"

IV's were in his arms, and the world was all swimmy. The room reeked with the smell of ketchup.

"Is the mask on too tight?" Dale said.

Harold felt for it, noticing the resemblance to the one back in that hospital in Iraq. He reached out for Dale's hand, took it.

"I love you, Son."

Dale sobbed. "We—we thought you were dead."

"We?"

Dale smiled.

"Mary?" Harold said.

"You finally awake?" Mary's voice came from across the room.

Dale looked down at his feet, shuffling them. "I got them to put you in the same room."

Harold reached out, feeling a little pain—the painkillers were doing a hell of a job—and pulled the curtain aside. He reached out for her, and their fingers touched.

"Harold, what I said back there—"

"It's okay, Mary. I know you don't—"

"I love you. Once we get out of here, we should give us a shot again."

Harold laughed, then regretted it. "Is that the drugs talking?"

"No. We can go back to the farm my Uncle Bruce had in the Smoky Mountains. Start over. What do you say?"

Dale rolled his eyes. "You two need to get a room. Pun intended."

They laughed.

Harold caressed her hand. "I love you so much."

"I love you, too."

"Son?" Harold said.

"Yeah, Dad?"

"Come here and give me a hug."

When they embraced, Harold could have sworn their hearts were in sync.

"Yo," Terrell said as he wheeled himself into the room. "Oh, thank God."

Harold tried to sit up, but the pain put him back down. "Terrell. Is that you?"

"Who else? When do we go home?"

Harold thought for a moment. "Do you like mountains?"

"Sounds good to me."

EPILOGUE

HAROLD SAT IN his rocking chair on the front porch of the farm, watching the sun turn the sparse clouds purple as it set. Green fields and forests at the base of the Smoky Mountains surrounded him. He signed the last letter and put it atop the rest on the small table beside him. Watching the wind ripple through the grass and hay soothed him. As a summer breeze hit him, he closed his eyes and inhaled the sweet air.

"Here we go," Mary said, walking out to join him with a glass of lemonade in her hand. "This is for you, honey."

Harold took it and sipped the sweetest lemonade he'd ever tasted. Then he sat his glass down, got up, and rubbed Mary's swollen belly. "I think it's gonna be a boy."

She laughed. "I hope it's a girl. I'll call her April."

Harold kissed her forehead. "I love that name."

"Dad?" Dale said, joining them.

"Yeah, Son?"

"How do I look for my date?"

Harold and Mary appraised him. He grew so fast that Harold's suit fit him just fine.

Mary smoothed Dale's hair back. "You're a lady killer. You have fun, sugar."

Dale blushed. "Thanks. I could use some clean air. Mind if I walk to Sarah's house?"

Harold beamed with pride. "Not at all. Have fun, and you treat her like a lady."

"Of course."

As Dale ran down the front lawn toward the road, Harold reached out and squeezed Mary's hand. "They grow up so fast. Don't they?"

Glowing, Mary pointed at the stack of letters. "What are those?"

"Finally got around to writing a letter to each family that lost their son or daughter back in Iraq when things went to shit that day."

Mary hugged him. "I'm so proud of you, love."

"Their families need to know that they fought bravely. When things got as bad as they could get, they died for *something*. Some of the smartest, toughest people I've ever known," Harold said, and squeezed Mary harder. Warm tears, healing tears, ran down his face.

She kissed him. "It's helping them heal, too."

Harold nodded his head. Then they stared at the Smoky Mountains.

Terrell opened the door and joined them. "Yo, now that's beautiful!"

Thunder rolled in the sky as the clouds darkened. The wind picked up, knocked the wind-chime off its hook. Harold picked it up and placed it by the door.

Mary walked down the steps, looked at the sky. "Looks like a bad storm is coming."

"We've seen worse," Harold said.

ACKNOWLEDGMENTS

Huge thanks go out to the amazing horror writers who took the time out of their busy schedules to give this novella hell: Patrick Rutigliano, Kenneth W. Cain, and John Palisano. The book wouldn't be the same without your expertise. My undying gratitude to Team Crystal Lake for believing in me and this story. Speaking of Team Crystal Lake, Bram Stoker Award Nominee, Monique Snyman did what every great editor does: she pushed me to my limits, making this book what it is today. To write is human, to edit is divine. Monique, you were divine.

And thanks to you, dear reader, for buying a copy.

Ben Eads
From the wilds of Florida
6/27/2019

ABOUT THE AUTHOR

Ben Eads lives within the semi-tropical suburbs of Central Florida. A true horror writer by heart, he wrote his first story at the tender age of ten. The look on the teacher's face when she read it was priceless. However, his classmates loved it! Ben's short fiction has appeared in magazines or anthologies by: Crystal Lake Publishing, *Shroud Magazine*, and Seventh Star Press. His first novella, *Cracked Sky*, was published in 2015 by the Bram Stoker Award® Winning press Omnium Gatherum. Ben blames Arthur Machen, H.P. Lovecraft, Jorge Luis Borges, J.G. Ballard, Philip K. Dick, and Stephen King for his addiction, and his need to push the envelope of fiction.

THE END?

Not quite . . .

Be sure to check out Ben Eads' *Cracked Sky!*

Or dive into more Tales from The Darkest Depths:

Novels:
Doll Crimes by Karen Runge
The Mourner's Cradle: A Widow's Journey by Tommy B. Smith
House of Sighs (with sequel novella) by Aaron Dries
The Final Cut by Jasper Bark
Blackwater Val by William Gorman
Nameless: The Darkness Comes by Mercedes M. Yardley

Novellas:
Every Foul Spirit by William Gorman
The Pale White by Chad Lutzke
A Season in Hell by Kenneth W. Cain
Quiet Places: A Novella of Cosmic Folk Horror by Jasper Bark
The Final Reconciliation by Todd Keisling
Run to Ground by Jasper Bark
Wind Chill by Patrick Rutigliano

Anthologies:
Shallow Waters Vol.3, edited by Joe Mynhardt
Tales from The Lake Vol.5, edited by Kenneth W. Cain
Fantastic Tales of Terror: History's Darkest Secrets, edited by Eugene Johnson

Welcome to The Show, edited by Doug Murano and Matt Hayward
Lost Highways: Dark Fictions From the Road, edited by D. Alexander Ward
C.H.U.D. Lives!—A Tribute Anthology
Behold! Oddities, Curiosities and Undefinable Wonders, edited by Doug Murano
Gutted: Beautiful Horror Stories, edited by Doug Murano and D. Alexander Ward

Short story collections:
Book Haven and Other Curiosities by Mark Allan Gunnells
Darker Days by Kenneth W. Cain
Dead Reckoning and Other Stories by Dino Parenti
Things You Need by Kevin Lucia
The Ghost Club: Newly Found Tales of Victorian Terror by William Meikle
Ugly Little Things: Collected Horrors by Todd Keisling
Whispered Echoes by Paul F. Olson
Embers: A Collection of Dark Fiction by Kenneth W. Cain

Poetry collections:
The Place of Broken Things by Linda D. Addison and Alessandro Manzetti
WAR by Alessandro Manzetti and Marge Simon
Brief Encounters with My Third Eye by Bruce Boston
No Mercy: Dark Poems by Alessandro Manzetti
Eden Underground: Poetry of Darkness by Alessandro Manzetti

If you've ever thought of becoming an author, we'd also like to recommend these non-fiction titles:

It's Alive: Bringing Your Nightmares to Life, edited by Eugene Johnson and Joe Mynhardt
The Dead Stage: The Journey from Page to Stage by Dan Weatherer
Where Nightmares Come From: The Art of Storytelling in the Horror Genre, edited by Joe Mynhardt and Eugene Johnson
Horror 101: The Way Forward, edited by Joe Mynhardt and Emma Audsley
Horror 201: The Silver Scream Vol.1 and *Vol.2*, edited by Joe Mynhardt and Emma Audsley
Modern Mythmakers: 35 interviews with Horror and Science Fiction Writers and Filmmakers by Michael McCarty
Writers On Writing: An Author's Guide Volumes 1,2,3, and 4, edited by Joe Mynhardt. Now also available in a Kindle and paperback omnibus.

Or check out other Crystal Lake Publishing books for more Tales from the Darkest Depths.

Hi readers,

It makes our day to know you reached the end of our book. Thank you so much. This is why we do what we do every single day.

Whether you found the book good or great, we'd love to hear what you thought. Please take a moment to leave a review on Amazon, Goodreads, or anywhere else readers visit. Reviews go a long way to helping a book sell, and will help us to continue publishing quality books. You can also share a photo of yourself holding this book with the hashtag #IGotMyCLPBook!

Thank you again for taking the time to journey with Crystal Lake Publishing.

We are also on . . .

Website:
www.crystallakepub.com

Be sure to sign up for our newsletter and receive three eBooks for free: http://eepurl.com/xfuKP

Books:
http://www.crystallakepub.com/book-table/

Twitter:
https://twitter.com/crystallakepub

Facebook:
https://www.facebook.com/Crystallakepublishing/

Instagram:
https://www.instagram.com/crystal_lake_publishing/

Patreon:
https://www.patreon.com/CLP

Or check out other Crystal Lake Publishing books for more Tales from the Darkest Depths. You can also subscribe to Crystal Lake Classics (http://eepurl.com/dn-1Q9), where you'll receive fortnightly info on all our books, starting all the way back at the beginning, with personal notes on every release. Or follow us on Patreon (https://www.patreon.com/CLP) for behind the scenes access, bonus short stories, polls, interviews, and if you're interested, author support.

With unmatched success since 2012, Crystal Lake Publishing has quickly become one of the world's leading indie publishers of Mystery, Thriller, and Suspense books with a Dark Fiction edge.

Crystal Lake Publishing puts integrity, honor, and respect at the forefront of our operations.

We strive for each book and outreach program that's launched to not only entertain and touch or comment on issues that affect our readers, but also to strengthen and support the Dark Fiction field and its authors.

Not only do we publish authors who are legends in the field and as hardworking as us, but we look for men and women who care about their readers and fellow human beings. We only publish the very best Dark Fiction, and look forward to launching many new careers.

We strive to know each and every one of our readers while building personal relationships with our authors, reviewers, bloggers, podcasters, bookstores, and libraries.

Crystal Lake Publishing is and will always be a beacon of what passion and dedication, combined with overwhelming teamwork and respect, can accomplish: unique fiction you can't find anywhere else.

We do not just publish books, we present you worlds within your world, doors within your mind from talented authors who sacrifice so much for a moment of your time.

This is what we believe in. What we stand for. This will be our legacy.

Welcome to Crystal Lake Publishing.

THANK YOU FOR PURCHASING THIS BOOK!

www.ingramcontent.com/pod-product-compliance
Lightning Source LLC
Chambersburg PA
CBHW051806050726
47598CB00006B/2447